NORTH OF THE GROVE

By William Hobbs

©2012

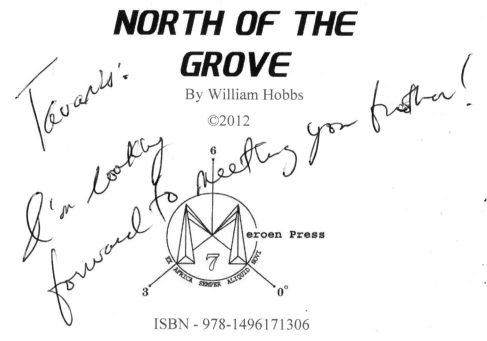

eroen Press

ISBN - 978-1496171306

Proceeds from the book go to completing the short film *North of the Grove*.

Special thanks to editors Wayne Christensen and Brianna Corbett

Northofthegrove.com / NOTGmovie@gmail.com

P.O. Box 824501

Pembroke Pines, FL 33082-4501

Phone: 1-954-861-0574

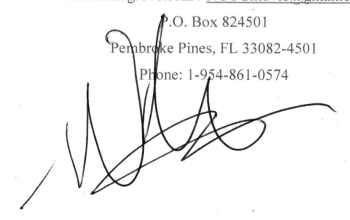

Dedication:

This is to my wife Dr. Tameka Bradley Hobbs, my co-partner in the grind to save minds, my brother, Bryan DeWayne Hobbs, now missing for 20 years and other young brothers struggling to find their way. Too human not to feel the loneliness, yet too scared to trust anyone that does come along. Everyone seems to wait for tragic circumstances to notice you, to categorize and condemn you for their own selfish purposes. You find yourself wanting to live and prosper not because it is your right to, but for the sweet and hateful purpose of embarrassing a world that minimized you at birth. Your existence is worth more than being fueled off such rage though. I know what's up. I am listening.

Chapter 1 - Ulterior

Howard Capelton

Professor Lovelett, I'm going to meet this kid in a week and my stomach is in knots! I feel so ashamed. People like that can tell when you're uncomfortable.

August 15

Victor Lovelett

People like that? Like what?

August 15

Howard Capelton

You know, the lower class people that need this program. The violent, loud kind that are even worse when you're black because they think all black people should be the way they are.

August 15

Victor Lovelett

Which is?

August 15

Howard Capelton

Raw. Ugly. Out-of-control.

August 17

Victor Lovelett

Lol.

August 18

Howard Capelton

I just want this mentoring thing to work so I can stand myself. If I can do that, I can calm down and she'll stop asking me so many questions. Then, this marriage and having kids "thing" can work out. I'm afraid of what will happen if this doesn't work. I've tried everything else.

August 18

Victor Lovelett

This should put you in the right direction. That 5000 Role Models group you joined was a good move. More black professionals need to reach back and help kids. So they hooked you up to volunteer with this in-home counseling service?

August 19

Howard Capelton

Yes. An invite came through my company email out of nowhere about the induction process. I had never heard of the organization before. You know I don't bother with all of that fraternity, organization stuff. I just keep to myself. Tiff said it would be good for me though so I went and they put me to work with this counseling situation fast! Lol. She thinks I'm doing this counseling just to get used to being around kids since she wants to get pregnant. Well, in a way I am.

August 19

Victor Lovelett

But?

August 21

Howard Capelton

More than anything, I have to do this to keep from jumping off of an overpass face-first.

August 21

Victor Lovelett

How long have you all been married?

August 21

Howard Capelton

Six years.

August 21

Victor Lovelett

I must say that a lot of my own recklessness slowed down after I had my first child. The key to the Africanized community mindset we used to discuss in class is getting beyond European selfishness and self-preservation to recognize how others need and value you. They may, at times, value you more than you value yourself.

August 22

Howard Capelton

Thank you for keeping my secret. I know you told me to stop thanking you, but when I typed the words thank you and saw them on the screen, it became easier for me to breathe. I think if this all works out with this kid, it won't sit on my shoulders and pick at my brain so much and I'll be able to get on with my life.
August 22

Victor Lovelett

I understand. I have an issue with discussing such sensitive information over Facebook. It was the one concern I had with "friending" you, wondering if after all this time, you were still struggling with this and would bring it up in this forum. Our discussion in my office when you were here at FAMU is one thing. Like you, I'm trying to be more community-oriented and help others beyond lectures, but I don't believe these Facebook Instant messages back and forth just disappear into thin air. You shouldn't either. Keep me posted on your meeting with the boy. Prepare for struggle, without it, there is no progress. It might also do you some good to write a journal for yourself about this mentoring experience.

August 22

 Sharia Troy

 David Troy

August 24, 2009

Journal:

I was told it would be good for me to write about my mentoring experience. Honestly, I believe I'm writing for you, Tiffany. If this mentoring with Sunrise Family Services doesn't work out and you learn more about me than I was ready to say, at the very least, this will give you more of the explanation I won't be around to give you. I scanned their pics. This is the mother, Sharia and her son, David. I doubt you'll ever meet them. This is how my initial meeting went.

I drove back to the old neighborhood in West Grove for the women's shelter. The presence of my people is still there. The vacant lots and boarded up windows cannot erase it. The spirit dances off the Africanized murals up and down Grand Ave. When the heat from the street gets caught in the breeze, in spite of the exhaust from passing cars, I still get a hint of it in the scent of cocoa buttered black skin, old houses and the leaves of tired palm and oak trees. You felt in the black restaurants, churches, dry cleaners, movie theatres next door or across the street from each other. We were doing it and it was even stronger with my dad's generation, when our Carver High School taught every black child in Miami. We had our own like the Cubans.

Ms. Cheney, the shelter's administrator, met me out front among the Pandora vines crawling out of control along the fence. Cheney, a hard-looking Jamaican lady, took me inside and introduced me to Sharia and David. I went over the specifics of Sunrise Family Services, which included a 24 hour intervention, seven days a week. I informed David and Sharia that there would be at least two face-to-face sessions every week. Cheney excused herself when an argument broke out in the main hall. In Cheney's absence, I went over how I would run mandatory weekly case management, which included school visits, contact with service providers and curfew checks. I stressed to Sharia and David the importance of cooperating with facilitating SFS sessions. Sharia's hair was in complete disarray. She sat in her chair laying her head in her hands and nodding at my questions. He sucked on a lollipop and sat in a chair pushed back away from us in the room. He kept his thick, dry arms folded and his eyes on his untied sneakers. Cheney returned. I asked to speak to Sharia and Cheney in private. He got out of his chair and proceeded to the door before I finished asking the question. Sharia pounded her thigh and asked David if anybody had informed him to move yet. He sucked his teeth and rolled his eyes. Sharia leaned forward in her chair in order to close the distance between then and hissed at him to give her "reason to"; that she wished he "would" (presumably give her a reason to hit David)... I thought she was going to lay him out. He remained still. Sharia warned him that if he made another move she would "stomp a hole" in him and "watch it dry." I told Sharia it was okay for him to go. David dragged his feet out of the room.

I addressed issues brought on by David witnessing Sharia's sexual assault due to a home break-in at the hands of two local males back in her hometown of Richmond, Virginia. I spoke of the file's saying he distrusted older men, teenage boys and authority figures. I spoke about reports of his hyperactivity and sudden rash of violent outbursts since the assault. Sharia huffed and commented that I "looked real bookish" and wondered if I could "just talk" him into not getting her kicked out of the shelter. I asked what she was talking about. Sharia explained that due to his fighting with the children at the afterschool program he attended, she and David were "liable to be put out." I looked at her in some kind of way I can't explain. I just remember thinking, "is that all you want to say?" Sharia apologized and said she knows David is just "acting out of what he might have saw" in regards to the assault. Sharia, Cheney and I agreed that most of his anger is from his inability to defend her. Sharia seemed to soften, somewhat. We talked of his violent outbursts in school, where he responded to playful behavior from other fourth graders with flurries of punches, kicks and then spitting, once the victim was on the ground.

I recalled reading in the case file of Sharia's attacker's spitting on David during her assault. I observed his recent schoolwork (he struggles in school and sucks in math). I asked Sharia if it was alright for me to talk with him alone for a while. Sharia got up and before walking out of the door, mentioned that he likes basketball. Then, I'm alone with him in a separate room, he appeared agitated and demanded I leave the door open.

I opened door and asked David how old he was. He said nine. I told him that I understand why he fights with classmates. I admitted that kids do annoying things. I admitted I had wanted to beat up a few people when I was a child, but refrained because it was not worth the trouble. He quickly countered by insisting grown-ups "do stupid junk, too." I asked if he meant how adults may stick up for people that annoy him. He remained silent. I explained that fighting is understandable in the right circumstances, but that swarming someone with kicks and punches to someone who did a little teasing, was rather excessive. I emphasized that such force makes people take the other person's side. I suggested he refrain from spitting on people because that was beneath the honor of a true warrior. David attempted to ask something, but I could not understand his words. I suggested he either throw out the lollipop or chew it up so his words would be understood.

David asked what the word honor meant. I stated that honor was a discussion for the future, but he could consider improving his fighting skills by learning karate or boxing (which would in turn stress discipline and self-restraint from spitting on people). He slowly chewed the lollipop, sat up and began to offer more eye contact. I re-emphasized that learning karate or boxing is about self-defense, not becoming a bully. I stood up and informed him that I would see him the next day and wanted to hear that he was doing better in school and with his mother. I attempted to pat him on the shoulder. He stepped back out of reach and told me I really did not need to "be doing all that" (physical contact). I agreed, but accidentally extended out my arm in order to shake his hand. David scratched his head and looked away as I withdrew my hand. I thanked him for his time and left.

Howard Capelton

I went on my lunch break to see him. The shelter was so dark! The mother is a drunk for sure. She was beaten and gang raped by her drug dealer ex-boyfriend's rivals. The boy's name is David and he saw way too much of what they did to her. His file says he was teased by others about what happened to his mother and became more violent. Sometimes he was violent to himself. Like licking 9 volt batteries for the sting, rubbing erasers into his arm for the burn, beating his head on his desk at school.

August 24

Victor Lovelett

You're not supposed to be telling me his actual name. That's confidential. I don't trust Facebook instant messaging, Howard.

August 24

Howard Capelton

Yeah, you're right. I'm messing up everything already.

August 24

Victor Lovelett

Watch him closely around sharp objects. He could be working his way to cutting.

August 24

Howard Capelton

It's like he hates himself for not being able to save her. He was only eight at the time and is ashamed that he could not fend off armed, grown men for his mother.

August 24

Victor Lovelett

It's amazing what children expect they should know and do at such an early age.

August 24

Howard Capelton

Thanks. I know what you mean. He seems to only half-way care what she says. Typical kid, I guess. His clothes smelled bad. His breath smelled worse. I don't even know how I can get to that subject with him. "Hello. Boy, are you brushing your teeth?" And he has this look in his eye. It's like he's not impressed or trusting of me as an adult. He told me adults do things just like kids.

August 24

Victor Lovelett

Adults have let him down.

August 24

Howard Capelton

And I won't? He already sees me as bookish, the mother, too.

August 24

Victor Lovelett

Bookish, meaning?

August 24

Howard Capelton

As in, not being a man. She actually said I was bookish-looking.

August 24

Victor Lovelett

There is a certain kind of masculinity they've seen around them, a narrow, specific type that has garnered respect thus far. They just need to see that black men have other ways to carry themselves and still get things done. They need to see your style of masculinity navigate through situations. It will broaden their world.

August 24

Howard Capelton

You make this sound easy.

August 24

Victor Lovelett

It isn't. No struggle, no progress.

August 24

Howard Capelton

I even suggested he try boxing or karate. Lol. I came up with that off the top of my head to get his attention. Self-defense initiatives aren't even in the program's budget. We have no community connections to help get him into any kind of class, not to mention waivers to consider in case of injuries. He's already violent. He could injure someone and it would be my fault.

August 24

Victor Lovelett

Okay, insurance man. Lol

August 24

Howard Capelton

Yeah, I gotta get back to work anyway. I'm in over my head promising things I can't deliver in order to connect with him. I'm already at a loss. I shouldn't have put that boxing stuff in the report. I don't know what I'll do if they make a big deal out of it.

August 24

Victor Lovelett

You'll do the work. You'll explain what needs explaining. Some things belong on record and some don't. It's funny how what doesn't belong on record is what's needed most these days. Just do the work, which is figuring out what's for the records and what isn't and be there for him. That's all you can do.

August 24

August 24

Tiff:

I know you have your counseling session after work. Just heard of some kind of drug-related shooting in that area where you said the boy lives. Be careful while you're out saving the world. Text me back on what you want for dinner.

1:34p.m.

He does live out there. I'll be alright.

1:51 p.m.

Tiff:

My hero ;)

2:03 p.m.

That's how I roll. I want some salt fish and dumplings. And bacon.

2:10 p.m.

August 24, 2009

Journal:

I rode by the old house in West Grove (I refuse to call it Village West). I had stayed up all night thinking about the grown folks' parties ma and dad threw in the living room. I thought about my old room and the plastic covering nailed onto the green bean-colored carpet through the hall. The new, periwinkle paint job helped the house, gave it new life under power lines that still hung with more slack than they did on Grand Ave. An older man walked out if it like it's just the house he happened to buy, nothing special. Like he never could imagine that the bedroom to the right, by the shrubs, was locked up from the rest of the family and life the neighborhood once had. I went down the old store fronts on Grand Ave, counting black light posts without Coconut Grove historical banners, past vacant lots and abandoned apartment buildings, AC units poking out of their boarded up windows. Barely fifty yards down the road stood the Cheesecake Factory, Fat Tuesdays, Starbucks of the polished CocoWalk, where spoiled UM students, tourists in Croc sandals and the silicone and botoxed well-to-do shop and act like they can't look to see all this just beyond the Post Office. This, the city of Miami's, and our own, neglect. I always grit my teeth at the brutal contrast, even though I am glad I have the means to be among them.

I got to the Fairchild After-School Program to meet with Sharia and David. He kept eye contact minimal and remained beyond arm's reach as though fearful I would touch him. I suggested we go to a nearby basketball court and shoot hoops (Yes, I know... *me and basketball*). David winced and asked if I knew how to play basketball. It reminded me of all I went through coming up over there. I had to say I could play well enough to beat him. I playfully jabbed him.

David went stiff. I instructed him to fix his shoes (he walks on the heels of his sneakers like they're sandals).He backed up before doing it as if to keep me from touching him. I walked him out to the car, opened the passenger door and presented him with a new basketball. He was hesitant about getting in until he saw the ball. He got into car and ran his fingers over the grain of the basketball. He commented on how new the ball smelled and then mentioned that he was going to lift weights so he could grip it with one hand one day. I joked that David needed to try weights "or something" since he was small for a fourth grader. He looked me like I was stupid.

I drove out of the parking lot and challenged David to a game. He reminded me that I had on "church shoes and pants." I asked if he was scared. He snickered and responded "nigga you silly." I hate to say it, but he speaks with this strength, this certainty, that annoys me. I informed David that there was no need to speak so disrespectfully just because he was going to lose. I made David buckle his seat belt and lock his door. I advised him to consider different ways of expressing himself so he wouldn't keep butting heads with Sharia and people at his school. I suggested he tell people when something's becoming a problem instead of holding it all in and exploding about it to the point that no one wants to hear his point of view. He remained silent and stared out of the window. I said the only way to know he has a good life is by the kind of relationships he has with people and relationships are handled by the way he communicates with others. Yes, I used something I heard you say.

David appeared to be stifling laughter. I asked what was so funny. He shook his head and informed me that I just said "relationship" and that "ladies and girls be saying that on TV." I went to the court at Virrick Park (since I still suspect it's toxic over there by Barnyard Community Center court where that Old Smokey incinerator used to be). Maybe that possible arsenic and cadmium in the soil's why the people seemed drained. I think of the Gibson Health Initiative on Grand Ave. Maybe they know how people have suffered and felt justified in protecting them with the tinted and mirrored windows out front that tell me to mind my damn business with my own reflection. Family practitioner Pierre Blemur's office is next door, with his MedPlus, Labcore and West Diagnostics drop boxes outside of his tinted doors. The Grove Pharmacy is still a short way down at the Douglas intersection. They all could be out on the main road to take care of the nosy, poor and aging that remain in West Grove. They could be there to fight what that incinerator, and a few other things, did to the whole community.

I say it's the people in general. Their tired, unfamiliar faces barely acknowledged me as they sat on wooden benches at bus stops, hung out at corners or moved along shuttered, vacant storefronts. Shirtless black men in sagging Dickie work pants and old school Converse high tops rode bikes at a pace that said they really had no place to go. It all seemed to help the overcast sky that swallowed up the modern buildings and palm trees. I called myself warming up with lay ups off the backboard. It had me thinking of the old days, of being laughed at for getting my first major erection listening to a Jam Pony Express DJ's mix of Too Live Crew records between pick-up games of football at Ambrister Park. That made me recall finding out, days after filming, that Michael

Jackson crept into town and filmed his *Thriller* video in our local cemetery, of imagining how it disturbed my little sister, even though I got a jheri curl like Jackson soon afterwards. That messy hairstyle blinded me so the day after Christmas when my Schwinn ten-speed was stolen off Plaza Street. I ran home in a dry-mouthed panic. Dad had warned me things were changing in the neighborhood, that I had better lock it up.

David informed me that other players on the court were looking at me "dressed like that." I said I would still beat him anyway. I did fairly well, beating him by one point to a game of ten without busting a sweat. I tried to impress him with almost gripping the ball with one hand. David ignored it to practice his dribbling and asked if I had to dress "like that" to see him. I said not really. He asked why then did I dress like that when "all these other niggas down here be in flip flops and shorts." I advised him to refer to people in a term other than the "n" word. I explained that I was Bahamian. I motioned to other players on the court, all whom were black, and stated that some could be Haitian, Jamaican or any of the other nationalities that are in the South Florida area. I stated that many black people from all over the world do not tolerate being called the "n" word. I offered that apples come in different forms; apple pie, apple juice, regular apples. David shot the basketball into the hoop without touching the rim and stated: "they still apples."

The funny thing is I feel the same way. The fools out there with stocking caps and gold teeth were the types that gave me way too many problems. Underwear poofed out over pants like pampers. You think I'm crazy but Chris Rock is a genius; there is a war between blacks and niggas. Yes, David, these are niggas, but I'm an adult so I have to lie. I have to be phony. And yet, even though I could be attacked and robbed by one of these thug bums, I preferred them around over one of those neighborhood elders with a good memory and too many questions.

David asked what job I had besides "seeing him." I said I was part of an organization called 5000 Role Models of Excellence Project. His eyes grew large. He asked if I really had "5000 dudes rolling" with me. I said "in a way" and that these "5000 dudes" are all intelligent brothers looking to help guys like him stay out of trouble, that they got me into doing what I was doing with him. He asked how I made money. I explained that I worked with an insurance company. He asked what was insurance. I explained that insurance is an agreement that someone help people if something bad happens to them. He passed the ball and asked "how insurance do that?" I said with money mostly. He said he never had insurance. I told him that I was in his life now and that was a start. He asked if that meant that I had to give him money. I stated no, explaining that I meant insurance as in he had someone to help him out when things got crazy.

David tried a behind the back pass to me and said insurance "sound like people making sure each other okay, like maybe a gang." I suggested he consider it as someone who has friends. He said Sharia "might could have insurance, but just don't." I asked why. He hesitated answering, stopped dribbling his ball for a moment and then asked if I "go give insurance money to people" when something happens. I stated that I determine how much money a family receives when, for instance, a family member is killed accidentally. He said that sounded like "too much" and asked if I "got rich" doing it. I shot the ball and assured him that I was far from being rich. He caught the ball and stated it did not look like I could "fight good," that I looked like people who "always hopin' somebody hold 'em back and break it up." I was smiling but I was pissed. I insisted that most people don't truly want to fight even when they get into it with others. David shot the ball in and stated, with dead seriousness, "I do."

I lied and assured David that I had a few scuffles "in my time." David asked what "in my time" meant. I explained it meant when I was younger, as in a teenager. He asked how old I was and I responded age thirty-five. He appeared confused and stated that men who look my age and even "high school boys" fight "everybody, even little kids sometimes" in his hometown of Richmond, Virginia. I escorted him back to the car. He remained silent and held tight to his new basketball. He then began to observe the dashboard and what was in the back seat and the car stereo. I smiled. He nodded as if tolerating the gesture. This boy has a strength in him I despise and admire. Where would I be now if I had had it back at such an early age?

I caught David taking special notice of a karate school as I drove back to Fairchild After-School Program Center. I thanked him for his time and ended the session. He ran quickly into the building with the basketball, as though fearful that I would ask for it back. I saw him at a window, clutching the basketball, watching as if to make sure I was driving off.

August 26, 2009

Journal:

I drove to Fairchild After-School Program to meet with Sharia and David. I discovered he had punched a kid in the ear for asking where he lived. He felt the kid was making fun of him and Sharia having to live in the shelter and, for some time, in their car. He greeted me with arms defiantly crossed and quickly stated that he did not have the basketball I had given him. I reassured him that I would not ask for the basketball back. I asked if he had people give things to him and take them back. He looked off and shrugged his shoulders. I suggested he walk with me outside so we could talk. He trailed behind, holding his hand as if he had hurt it. I instructed him to stop walking on the backs of his shoes and asked exactly what the boy had said that was so troubling. He stated the boy, Effrom, was constantly "talkin' mess about people anyway" so when he asked David where did he "stay" and continued to ask even after David said "around," he thought peer was "tryin'" him. He yelled that everybody knows that when people say "around" it means "things ain't good" and that people do not want to talk about it.

I suggested that David say "none of your business" instead of punching people. He said he "sort of" did when he informed Effrom to get out of his face. He said Effrom asked again, and said that he thought he had seen David playing basketball near a crack house. I reminded him that he was playing basketball at a nearby court – with me – yesterday, in fact. He stated that Effrom "got this smile all the time like something's funny" and that he "just couldn't take it no more." He stated that he hates when people whose clothes are "all new and good" and smell "all flowery like yours (mine)" ask questions about his "business." He stated that they don't care and "just ask to show you you ain't like them." I told him that the first part about having good clothes is taking care of them and that walking on the backs of his shoes only break down his shoes and make them look as crappy as those people want him to feel. I asked if he thought I asked him things to make him feel bad. He took out a box of Airhead candy, emptied half the box into his mouth and mumbled something under his breath. This boy eats way too much candy.

I asked David if he remembered that I could help him get boxing or karate lessons if he behaved. He suggested I say "stay out of trouble" because "behaved is for babies and dogs." I informed him that I planned to take him out to play more basketball and do different things of that sort, but could not if he continued to get into trouble. David reminded me that I "can't play none noway." He then straightened his posture, swallowed the candy and said since Effrom did not try to hit him back, that it was not "really really" a fight, just "a hit." He said he did "not even spit" on Effrom "either." I agreed that there are rude people who don't deserve what they have and who say and do harmful things. I re-emphasized that he must deal with people who "try" him in equal measure with what they do, so a possibly innocent question does not deserve such a "hit." He asked what about adults that "try" him.

I asked David which adult does that to him. He grew tight-lipped and shook his box of candy. I informed him to let Sharia handle adults who "try" him. He gave a pained expression. I asked him to go up to a nearby window of the building and point out peer. He picked candy out of his teeth and walked to a window. He stood on the tip of his toes and pointed Effrom out. I asked if he noticed that Effrom has this funny-shaped head. He smirked and, between trying to keep his mouth closed and chewing more of the candy, agreed Effrom "kinda did" and that it was "all long in the back like the hooky part on a hammer." I suggested that Effrom may not have been trying to be funny but, if Effrom ever did, that he keep that "hook hammer head of his" in mind and joke about it with peer. David said all he ever noticed was Effrom's nice clothes and nasty smile. I walked him back into the building and complimented him on his honesty, to which he squirmed. I concluded the session. David did not watch from the window.

August 27

Tiff:

Enjoyed last night.

1:09 p.m.

Yeah. I know.

1:13 p.m

Tiff:

Jerk. ;)

1:30 p.m.

Tiff:

Did you enjoy last night?

1:45 p.m.

Yeah. Why?

1:50 p.m.

Tiff:

Because I want to know if I make you happy. You never share how you feel about me. You never share how well I do what I do... why?

1:57 p.m.

Lol. Guess I focus mainly on you being happy and just leave it at that.

2:03 p.m.

Tiff:

Don't leave it. Ever. I'm trying to make it so that you can't even imagine leaving it.

2:05 p.m.

Howard Capelton

Would you believe I was out playing basketball with him? I figured I should try to get him going with some sport not as violent as karate and boxing. He's still sniffing me out, like they all do.

August 27

Victor Lovelett

Sniffing you out? I don't follow.

August 27

Howard Capelton

You know, sizing me up. Seeing if I'm soft. The other guys on the court were doing it, too. Like they wanted to see if I was jackable. Tiff doesn't even think I can handle this. I can tell from her "be careful" comments. I came home and she acted like I was some vet from Iraq.

August 27

Victor Lovelette

Jackable?

August 27

Howard Capelton

Jackable as in being jacked, as in getting robbed. We were in West Grove. I don't know what I was thinking.

August 27

Victor Lovelett

A little confidence and common sense on your part will go a long way. When I was in grad school at Northeastern in Chicago, I was walking down a street one night and picked up on a dude walking in my direction. I sensed his intentions and immediately straightened up my back. I made a point of looking him in his eyes as he came close enough to pass me. His mouth just dropped like he was tongue-tied, like he was used to people looking away to make it easy for him. He was bigger than me and the whole nine, but it didn't matter. I walked off in a cold sweat but with my wallet and life intact. August 27

Howard Capelton

Imagine if I had gotten robbed or something by them in front of this boy. He called me a silly nigga because I had my clothes from work on. I don't even own a pair of basketball sneakers! I think I was talking too much. I told him it was important for him to work on his relationship with his mother. He basically called me soft for using the word relationship. He said only females use that word. He's still in elementary school and ready to tell me what macho's all about, at least in his world. He even said it didn't look like I know how to fight.

August 27

Victor Lovelett

You've got an interesting situation! Lol. I thought about you and this kid while I was in church the other day. "Train up a child in the way he should go; even when he is old he will not depart from it."

August 27

Howard Capelton

Let's hope so. The sad part is, I might have to get kind of street in my approach. The same 'hood crap I've hated all my life. It amazes me that I have to get a gold tooth in my mouth, and some record with the police before a kid will listen to me. I guess people, especially men, who know better than to get into all that street crap from the beginning can't reach kids.

August 27

Victor Lovelette

I've struggled with that one, too. At least you're young. All they see in me is some old man that wandered out of a barbershop talking like he hates his own grandchildren. I speak at some of the rougher high schools and kids are on their phones or have headphones in their ears the whole time. Such disrespect. I'm hoping to learn ways to reach them through your experiences as well.

August 27

Howard Capelton

I did get a little street with him, actually. It pissed me off that he said all that stuff so I used the aggression to beat him at the basketball game. All these dudes were around looking at me like I was an idiot. Some guy cracked a joke about me and the kid froze with the ball in his hands, waiting to see what I would do.

August 27

Victor Lovelett

What did you do?

August 27

Howard Capelton

I heard another guy with him say at least I was there with my kid and then he asked the guy cracking jokes if he knew where his little girl was. Everybody laughed except the guy cracking jokes who started cursing everybody out. He started getting loud so I finished up the game and left.

August 27

Victor Lovelett

Crisis averted.

August 27

Howard Capelton

Not really by anything I did. I don't know. I think he wanted to see me react to the guy, to confront him. I was afraid to get into any more enlightened talk of how to handle things with people so I acted like I didn't hear what was being said.

August 27

Victor Lovelette

I thought you said you do neighborhood watch in your community? Lol

August 27

Howard Capelton

That's nothing. It's a gated community. Nothing really happens in gated communities. I jog with my cell phone. If kids are smoking or drinking by the playground or basketball court, if some couple's arguing too much by the lake, or somebody's by the clubhouse afterhours, I call security, period. I don't even break my stride. That's all I do, call while jogging. I only volunteered for that mess so these white folks out here can calm down and treat me like a neighbor instead of a suspect.

August 27

Victor Lovelett

Good luck with that. As far as merely talking theory about confrontations, being able to do that won't last for long. Eventually, he's going to want to know your perspective on how to handle direct confrontations.

August 27

Howard Capelton

He asked me about my job though. That was fun. I just can't let him and his environment rattle me. I just can't let that hood element in him annoy me to the point of forgetting he's just human.

August 27

Victor Lovelett

Everybody in his environment, your old neighborhood, is human, Howard.

August 27

Howard Capelton

Yeah. When I saw him yesterday, he had punched this boy in the head for asking him where he lived! Actually, I think the boy was just trying to get to know him. I could tell his hand was hurting, but he kept his cool.

August 27

Victor Lovelette

He's a soldier. He's hardened from witnessing what happened to his mother. And since older males like yourself committed the crime, he'll be looking for (and possibly be repulsed by) signs of strength and compassion in you for him to respond to.

August 27

Howard Capelton

He can tell his clothes don't smell too good either. He said people with clothes that smell good who ask questions about him are usually doing it to make him feel inferior. He was really pissed off, but I used the bait of karate/boxing to keep him focused. He said sometimes it's not kids that ask questions to make him feel low, that it's adults. I told him to let his mother handle the adults, forgetting that he witnessed his mother being assaulted by adults. You should have seen the pained expression on his face. I've got a lot to learn in a hurry.

August 27

Victor Lovelett

You're up to the challenge. You prove your strength and compassion by returning each day.

August 27

Howard Capelton

How'd you learn so much?

August 27

Victor Lovelett

You forget that I'm from Cherry Hill in Baltimore. I'm from a single parent home, so much so that I still cannot stand that "Rolling Stone" Temptations song. A lot of what I've learned came, unfortunately, the hard way.

August 27

Man, woman robbed in home, then detained when cops find marijuana and guns inside

August 27, 2009

(AP) A man and woman living in West Coconut Grove were robbed at gunpoint in their home early this morning and then detained when officers found dozens of marijuana plants and guns inside, a police spokesman said. The robbery occurred at about 1:48 a.m. at a home in the 200 block of 30th Avenue. The 28-year-old woman and 33-year-old man were at home when three suspects stormed in through a back door and robbed them at gunpoint, according to police.

According to the victims, the robbers took a registered assault rifle, an iPad, three cell phones and cash. Officers responding to the robbery then found 26 marijuana plants and 14 hand guns inside the home and detained the man and woman, police spokesman Lt. Charles Howard said. The names of the pair were not immediately available, but have been arrested, Howard said.

Paraphernalia on the premises indicated marijuana was being sold, Howard said. The robbers had not been found as of this morning and are believed to be part of a new scourge of gang activity in the area looking to get into drug dealing. They are described as three black men and "were more than likely known to the victims," Howard said. The black men are described as being 5 feet, 10 inches tall and weighing about 170 pounds, 6 feet tall and 200 pounds, 5 feet, 8 inches tall and weighing 175 pounds, according to Howard. Anyone with information about the robbery is asked to call the Police Department's anonymous tip line.

Chapter 2 – The Code

August 28, 2009

Journal:

I thought about how I'd deal with helping David decrease his hyperactivity as I drove to Green Garden Shelter for Women. Sharia greeted me at the door with her breath smelling like Listerine and looking more alert than the previous meeting. She claimed to be getting an apartment off Charles Ave.

While David was finishing his homework in another room, Sharia decided to fill in some blanks I had about how they got to where they were. She had been living in Richmond, Virginia with him and trying to establish a relationship with his father, who has not been a constant part of his life. The guy was involved in selling drugs and cheated someone out of money. He left her and David and apparently the people he cheated broke into her apartment and sought revenge by ransacking their belongings, breaking several of David's ribs and assaulting her sexually.

Sharia contacted an aunt here in Coconut Grove, Florida who suggested she move here to "get it together." Sharia stated that there was too much friction between herself and the aunt's husband, so she wound up sleeping in her car with David for two weeks until she found the shelter. I asked what the nature of the friction was. Sharia said "rent" and mumbled that the rest was a long story. I explained to Sharia that I was in no rush and sat down to hear the explanation. Sharia was taken aback. She said "all that" was all behind her anyway now that she had found an apartment for her and her son. I suspect it was some sexual tension, where she's laid around in the kind of cut offs she had on at the moment and things got rough with an older woman trying to divert her man's attention from it. Sharia is good-looking, but the problems that come with her can't be worth it.

Sharia interrupted me congratulating her on the apartment to say that David said I was supposed to be taking him someplace. I attempted to comment but Sharia again interrupted stating that his shoes were even on "the right way." He came out of the room with his finished homework and the basketball I had given him. He had scrawled his name across it with a permanent marker. He was chewing what looked like a full pack of bubble gum and seemed jittery. Upon realizing I was ready to leave for our community outing, he looked around as if to be certain others noticed. He dribbled the ball and said he would see several other kids later in a rather loud voice as I walked him to the car. I asked him what the reason for the volume was. He said nothing and nodded as if having difficulty focusing on what I was saying. I insisted he wear his seat belt. He laughed and said I was funny. I insisted again. He put on his seat belt and mumbled that doing so was "weird." I stated that children need to be protected and safe at all times when I'm in charge. I took him to the Books-A-Million bookstore. He drummed his fingertips over the basketball and nodded to music until he realized he had misheard the name of the place I was taking him (he thought I had said something along the lines of boxing million). David dragged his feet as he walked into the store.

We went into the café section of the store. I bought us smoothies. David swallowed his wad of gum before I could suggest he throw it out. He continued to speak at a volume better suited for being outside. I pulled out a homemade sandwich, sat with him and reminded him about using an inside voice. I presented him with a Jenga game and said if he could beat me a few times at it and read a story to me I would think about taking him to a boxing gym. I built a tower with the Jenga wood pieces. I explained that the objective was to take pieces out of the tower structure, one at a time, without making the tower fall and that whoever made the tower fall loses the game. I noticed he had difficulty keeping his hands steady. Because of this, he continued to knock down the Jenga tower, to which he tended to overreact by kicking chair legs, huffing too loudly or yelling. I made more of a point of praising him whenever he did pull a block out of the tower without knocking it over. After he had knocked the tower over for a third time, I praised David for pulling more blocks from the tower each time. He did not seem to notice, complaining that my hands, because of my BLT sandwich, had the pieces smelling like bacon. I picked a "Clifford the Dog" book out for him. David looked through the book and read it fairly well.

I praised David for reading so well and put my hand out to give him dap. This idiot asked if I was gay! I said no, but wondered what in the book brought up that question. He said men don't make boys wear seat belts, shake their hands or pat them on the shoulder or compliment them "so much like that." He explained that only mothers, grandmothers and "white lady teachers" are supposed to do that. I kept my cool and said he has a very interesting way seeing how things are supposed to be, being that he was only a child. I asked if "black lady teachers" compliment him. He said "a little," but that they get "mad quicker, too." I cleaned up the Jenga pieces and informed him that it was "cool" for a man to tell a boy "good job" sometimes, that fathers should do that for their sons. I drove him back to the shelter, twitching inside from anger. He asked if I would look into boxing or karate for him now. I made David pull up the back of his shoes and said I'd check out some places. I pulled into the Green Garden shelter and thanked him for behaving himself. He nodded, squirmed and said I could say something like "see you later" next time or maybe give him "a pound" instead. David demonstrated a "pound" (one person's fist pounding another in a hammer-to-nail fashion). I stated that I was raised calling such an expression giving someone "dap." I gave David dap, got in the car and didn't look back.

Howard Capelton

His mother's such a drunk. She could be kind of fine, if you get past her fake ponytail and those ugly house shoes she wears. I can see why the guys figured getting on her was a better payback than anything else.

August 28

Victor Lovelett

Watch what you say. She was assaulted and raped by them. Most dealers shoot people as payback.

August 28

Howard Capelton

Oh. The alcohol has ruined the only family relation she has in South Florida, bad move for somebody moving all the way from Virginia. She's supposed to be moving out of the shelter and in an apartment soon. I'll really be able to see what this kid has to deal with living with her then. It can't be good. He pulls at his shirt sleeves and walks on the back of his shoes, even decent–looking shoes. It's like he's uncomfortable with having nice things. And she feeds him constant sugary trash. He's bragging about me, too, sort of. He announced to the kids that he was about to go somewhere with me as we left.

August 28

Victor Lovelett

Not that many kids see a man your age taking interest in them. Sad but true. Of course he felt special.

August 28

Howard Capelton

He was so hopped up on sugar that he was knocking stuff over and fidgeting like crazy in the bookstore. It wasn't your typical restless kid stuff. He really is getting too much sugar in his diet.

August 28

 Victor Lovelett

Break it to the mother carefully.

August 28

 Howard Capelton

He asked if I was gay because I made him wear a seat belt! Everything that has to do with me being concerned with his safety's going to be considered gay to him! I'm in the business of insurance. I think safety all the time!

August 28

 Victor Lovelett

Many kids attribute manliness to a sense of recklessness, especially young manhood.

August 28

Howard Capelton

Then he figured I was gay because I complimented him on settling down and reading a book. He said only women pat him on the shoulder. Are men only allowed to curse, drink Hennessey and get into fist fights at street corners?

August 28

Victor Lovelett

White men can be anything they want. Only black men seem to be forced into this small existence of being "street" as you say.

August 28

Howard Capelton

Yes, everything else is gay, for us. I can see why dudes walk around mad in a way now. They could be pissed off at everything they're not supposed to be, allowed to be, enjoy or experience.

August 28

Victor Lovelett

Don't take it personal. Be creative. Black men in impoverished environments can express themselves. You just have to know the code that's accepted there. The problem is we as a people are stretched across these socio-economic spheres and middle class blacks don't care to understand the code of those struggling beneath them and vice versa.
August 28

Howard Capelton

He said it would be okay if I give him dap. Lol
August 28

Victor Lovelett

Give him dap, all that he can stand. He's already appreciating you coming to see him, even if it's for ulterior motives. Build from there.
August 28

Howard Capelton

But I can tell his mom thinks the same limited way about black men. I can tell by that bookish comment she made about me. How can I persuade him to be the kind of man she doesn't even respect or respond to? How can I persuade any boy to be more than black women appreciate? He's already clear on knowing that what people do and say are totally different.

August 28

Victor Lovelett

Lol. You said a mouthful right there. He's already in a mode to accept not what's right, but what works. It comes with being traumatized and the desperation that can follow. At the end of the day, this boy feels that being strong is the answer.

August 28

Howard Capelton

He might get that from her too, in a way. Her file says she hasn't taken any therapy or anything since her rape as if it was some sprained ankle she's trying to walk off.
August 28

Victor Lovelett

Yes. She's trying to be strong. She needs help. Let your supervisor consider how to approach her about that. As raggedy as she may seem, she's considering her son's welfare and mental health over her own. Her alcoholism is code. As I said before, the more you work with them, the more you'll see they're not statistics but humans being.
August 28

Howard Capelton

And she might drink out of guilt for putting him in such a bad situation. Having boyfriends who sell dope's asking for trouble. Humans being. Interesting typo. Lol
August 28

Victor Lovelett

That wasn't a typo.

August 28

August 29, 2009

Journal:

When I got to the shelter to pick up David, Sharia greeted me barefoot in an R. Kelly T-shirt and flowery pajama bottoms, happy to report that they would be moved into their apartment by late next week. She said that he had been acting quite well and could not stop talking about "karate and boxing." He was still having difficulty with several children at school and the after-school program. I stated that his restlessness may play a part in that.

Sharia said she "guessed so" and stated that David "can't keep still to save his life" but if he "plays basketball or something like that" with well-adjusted boys his age, he works it off. I discussed the role sugar in diet plays in hyperactivity with children. Sharia appeared to tense up as she said that she did "kinda" live in a shelter and that the community could not be as nice as wherever I must live. Sharia asked where I "stay." I stated that I *lived* in Miami, west of Kendall.

"Oh," Sharia almost laughed, "you stay where the white folks at." Sharia shared that, as with most "'hoods," there was not a decent grocery store nearby so people in the area are "stuck with Honey Buns and pickled eggs" over-priced convenient stores offer. I offered that Coconut Grove still has people all over that sell mangoes, coconut water and things of that nature for a change of pace. Sharia quickly retorted that she was from Virginia and "don't know nothin' 'bout that island monkey mess." I said I would try to bring oranges or bananas for David when he comes by and that statistics showed that children are now developing diabetes at a rate that gives them a better chance of being buried by their parents. Sharia snorted as if fresh fruits were something for animals to be fed. She appeared to try to force herself to relax. "Mr. Insurance Man, you and your big numbers."

Sharia admitted she could use a good sardine and cracker sandwich. She eyed me as if to see if such a sandwich would be considered healthy. She informed me that sardines are good for the heart and have more potassium than bananas. I nodded and said how my own grandmother can "get busy" with a sardine and cracker sandwich, although she undid most of its nutritional benefits with too much hot sauce. She asked me where my people came from, in a way that sounded like I wasn't completely "black." I told her I was Bahamian on both sides, from pioneer West Grovites, that both sides came from the Bahamas, one to do service work as the tourist trade started in the late 1800's, the other to build Flagler Memorial Bridge in the 30's.

I said how my grandfather lived off Grand Ave in the shanties with no running water or electricity. I was about to tell her how he wooed grandma, a woman whose family was among the first black settlers here for service jobs at the old Peacock Inn, with a bushel of sapodillas as she walked down Grand Ave. Like most niggas, most "apples", Sharia had tuned out to the moment in history by then. Black Americans disgust me. She asked me when the last time I went to the Bahamas was. I said eight years ago. Then she says, "So you stay south of the Grove. You act like you *north* of Grove." She then screamed for David to hurry on out, that "Prince Zamunda" (from *Coming to America* movie) was here to see him. Niggas disgust me.

David came up from one of the back rooms. Cheney followed behind him, saying that they had just finished a talk about David being respectful to adults when speaking to them. He attempted to quiet Cheney with agreeing, as though not to upset me. David apologized to Cheney and asked if I was ready to go.

I took David to several karate "dojos" (building where karate practitioners train with instructor). I spoke with the instructor to get the necessary information as the class stretched and warmed up. The instructor stressed the importance of concentration and focus. David interrupted several times to ask instructor to "make 'em start kickin' stuff."

I had him sit in a seated position with the class and meditate with them in order to focus. He kept fidgeting and giggling.

David was highly animated, karate kicking me in the legs as we walked back to the car. I chastised him about not buckling his seat belt and about horseplay, emphasizing that such recklessness would get him thrown out of a dojo. He buckled his seat belt and asked if I ever "played basketball or football for real." I shared that I ran 25K marathons. He stated that I was "skinny like that" and asked if I really "ran in the street all day long with all those white people." I said yes and that there are many types of people that run, in fact some of the best were Kenyans. I made the "A" sound, expecting him to finish the word African. David finished by stating the word, "apples" instead. He asked why, and how can people really see me since all those other people are in the way. I stated that I did not run for other people, only myself. He suggested I could run "a long ways" to a gym and do something "more cool" like "lift weights." He asked if white people told me to "go on somewhere" when I run near them. I assured him that not all white people were disrespectful. I pulled over to the beach and sat with him in the sand. We sat in the position used in the dojo. I instructed him to meditate to show he could be focused. His light demeanor quickly vanished when he realized I was serious.

David said I "ain't thinkin'" because homeless people who were nearby on benches could "just crack our ribs up 'cause our eyes closed." I had not noticed the homeless people. I remembered David having some ribs broken during his mother's rape and assault. He muttered meditating was "dumb" because there was not a safe place "anywhere – ever" to close one's eyes "this long." I got him back in the car, thanked him for being aware and told him to start practicing meditation when he sat on the toilet if he has to, that he needed to show that he could sit still and meditate for four minutes straight "like the karate people" before he could get into a class. I took him back to the shelter and thanked him for his enthusiasm and quick thinking at the beach. I attempted to give him "dap." Still rattled from the beach, he ignored my hand, nodded and hurried inside.

August 31, 2009

Journal:

I drove to Fairchild After-School Program and met with Mr. Sanford, the fifty-something year-old administrator of the after-school program. Sanford said he had to separate David and Effrom. Sanford assured me that the conflict between Effrom and David was just as much Effrom's fault in provoking conflict as it was David's intense, overly aggressive reactions. Sanford explained that David's screaming, punching, spitting, kicking and use of pencils as weapons tends to overshadow Effrom's part in the conflict when adults intervene. This angers David even more and puts him even more of an hostile, uncooperative mood. Sanford shared that Sharia's reaction to the situation (usually screaming, hitting David or grabbing him by his shirt and shaking him in front of everyone) makes him "absolutely impossible" for days at a time. Sanford stated that when he gets to that point, he will either go into a backpack-slinging, chair-throwing rage or appear to go without sleep, in which he will only communicate with shrugs, refuse food and water and tearfully draw highly developed pictures of women "in red." He showed me a picture. The woman was naked and covered in blood. Sanford stated he had been praised for his artistic talent but gets into trouble from drawing such disturbing pictures.

I thanked Sanford for the information and greeted David, who dragged his backpack and refused to look me in the eye. We got into car and I asked him what was wrong. He buckled his seat belt, folded his arms and shook his head. I drove to a local boxing gym. I playfully threatened him to talk about what was bothering him or else I would take him back to the beach to meditate with the homeless people. His face remained tense and fixed. I played some jazz music and shared information about the artist Cannonball Adderley. He remained silent. I talked about how careless kids are, that one day when they get older, they realize some of the things they've done to others and if they're decent people, they try to make up for it. I pulled into the parking lot of the boxing gym and told him that we would not get out of the car until he either meditated with me or started talking. He wiped a tear from his eye, locked his door and began to breathe deeply for meditation. He folded his arms and closed his eyes. A woman walked past the car and his eyes immediately opened. I kidded him, saying the woman was too old. He pounded the side panel. I reprimanded him. He snapped that it "ain't that good a car no way." David unbuckled seat belt, began to bawl and kicked the floor mat. I patted him on the back. He tensed up. I withdrew my hand. Why do women want kids?

David screamed that he hated "everybody." He claimed that everybody "can do stuff to me and I can't do nothin' back." I assured him that he could do something. I said that first off, instead of exploding on Effrom when provoked, he needed to let an adult know what Effrom was doing by saying "excuse me, I'm trying to be cool but this boy keeps messin' with me." I explained that if he did that, it would be the adult's job to set Effrom straight. If the adult didn't and he got mad when Effrom did it again, then at least he would have warned everybody. David lifted his head somewhat and began wiping his nose. I took David into the boxing gym. His face dried as he watched two boxers spar in the ring. After speaking with the gym's manager, I put gloves on him and showed him how to ball his fists for a good punch. He seemed to look over my shoulder at the trainer, as if to not respect that I would know anything about self-defense. It took everything in me not to walk out and leave. I noticed his shoes, told him to stop treating them like "flip flops" (standing on the backs of his shoes) and then placed David in front of a kiddie-sized punching bag.

I then suggested David think of everyone that got on his nerves (I guess the way I was thinking he and his mother were getting on mine). He began swinging wildly. I barked at him to punch harder. I yelled as if he was hitting me through the bag. I wanted to see him worn out. He grinned and continued until he gasped between punches. Exhausted, he leaned on the bag, hugging it and said that he didn't care, that one day, he'd leave and his mother would "wish she was dead." I wanted to hug the bag, too. Not sure why. I took the gloves off him. He sighed as if he had gotten a huge weight off his shoulders. I drove him back playing jazz. I got him a bacon burger through a Burger King drive-thru. He fell fast asleep, didn't even open the bag. I reached the after-school program, woke him up, and complimented him on his right hook. David did not complain, opting to focus on getting his burger and fries out in one piece. He slammed the door shut as I reminded him of what to do if Effrom started "tripping" again.

Chapter 3 – The Blackness

 Howard Capelton

The mother did seem somewhat knowledgeable of nutrition in a stank kind of way. She tried to clown me for living in a quiet, safe part of town. It's like she was saying any area that's clean and safe must be white because black people are supposed to live in chaos. Fools like living in foolishness even if their kids wind up suffering for it.

August 31

 Victor Lovelett

Is it still being taken over by the other folks? I used to go there and enjoy their Goombay Festivals. I hear that they don't get money from the city anymore to have them in order to phase them out. Gentrification. I remember you telling me they demolished West Grove buildings to house trolleys that only serve Coral Gables. You may be seen by his mother as someone who happily sided with the white folks.

August 31

Howard Capelton

I guess so. I told her where I lived, that its south of the Grove. She said I act like I'm
north of the Grove. I suspect she means as in I think I'm better than what it has become,
like it's supposed to be what it is now. She doesn't seem committed to black communities
per se. She seems committed to 'hood drama. I don't know. I hate blackness being
equated with low standards of living.
August 31

 Victor Lovelett

I'm with you on that one. It's just challenging to articulate that in a way that's
understood.
August 31

 Howard Capelton

If that's what being black is to her she can keep it and I will be teaching her son to be in
complete disagreement with that. The kid was hyped about karate like I feared. I talked
to my supervisor and was told that there is a community program by a YMCA out here

that would allow him to take classes. I don't know what I got myself into with this. It was so embarrassing when we got there to observe a class. He went in there acting like Madea in those Tyler Perry movies, all loud, telling the karate instructor to make the students stop stretching and fight so he can see it. And he's testing me again, too, telling me my marathon running is not cool, that I should lift weights. He won't be happy until I'm on steroids, sagging my pants and full of tattoos. It's really testing my patience. It's like he's saying "be like this so I can really show you off, so I can genuinely be proud of you." I'm thinking, your father abandoned you from the get-go, boy. You're getting your head beat in from situations your mother's put you in from her hoodrat choices for boyfriends to make up for his absence. I've stepped up to help so who are you to be choosey? To make it worse, I took him to the beach to teach him how to meditate, to calm down and focus. He was more alert to the environment than I was. He noticed homeless people nearby and assessed the possible threat of them attacking us while our eyes were closed. I felt like I was the child and he was the adult. If you can't relax at a beach though, where can you? If I wanted to meditate in the park by my subdivision, I would think nothing of it.

September 1

Victor Lovelett

Hoodrat and all of those terms. Be careful of them. They're lazy ways of writing a person off as a type, instead of knowing them for yourself. Besides, he lives in a reality that's different from yours. And don't do that better-than American black, Caribbean/Bahamian mess to them! LOL. The Bahamas is considered one of the most dangerous places in the Caribbean these days!

September 1

Howard Capelton

You just had to bring that up, huh? LOL. I want to take him to my park, so he can see how clean and inviting it is so I don't look like some idiot to him for having suggested meditating in one, but he was so freaked out by the book store. The whispering voices, the calm jazz playing was flipping him out! Tiff's against bringing him into our neighborhood. She's saying be careful or the kid could become too attached since I'm only supposed to be working with this kid for a year or two maximum.
September 1

Victor Lovelett

Ah, and how is your wife Tiffany responding to all of this?
September 1

Howard Capelton

Tiff likes when I come home and talk about the stuff he does – to a point. She applauds it, even tells her colleagues at Pfizer about it like we're some well-to-do family taking in some international student from abroad. I can tell she just wants to see that side of me fully developed so that she can cut my ties with this boy and be ready to have kids. Forever plotting.

September 1

Victor Lovelett

Yin and yang, my friend.

September 1

Howard Capelton

I'm going to take him to a nice park, one day. Some black people are afraid that they're not even worth living in such calm, that they're not worth having such peace of mind. I gotta help him with his temper, too (even more of a reason for him to learn how to meditate). Kids antagonize him and when he explodes on them, he goes so over the top with it that it's easy for people to disregard what the other kid did and just jump all over him. He blew up about it in my car about how unfair it is. I was told by the after-school administrator that he gets mad sometimes and draws these pictures of naked women covered with blood.

August 31

 Victor Lovelett

You know who that is he's drawing, right?

September 1

 Howard Capelton

Yep, it's Sharia. I don't know what to do about it yet.

September 1

 Victor Lovelett

If the mother is as proud as I think she is, she's trained him not to tell any of their personal business to people. I bet when she's clear-headed she goes over with him whatever he shares with you in order to control what is being revealed. Opening up to you, an authority in an agency, is probably one of the most stressful things they've attempted. It could be another filter by which they view your blackness as being questionable.

September 1

Howard Capelton

I took him to a boxing gym and let him punch on a punching bag. I told him to think of everyone that annoys him. He tired himself out and slept hard on the ride back. Guess that's a way of getting it out without words. The code. Lol
September 1

 Victor Lovelett

Isn't it amazing, the world a kid like that has to deal with and keep to himself?
September 1

September 2
Mr. Capelton:

I'm just e-mailing you to say I'm quite pleased with the feedback from David's after-school program about you. The program administrator knows a reporter for the *Dade County Gazette* that would be interested in doing an article, but David's mother did not want to be bothered. That would really be ideal publicity for us and your 5000 Role Models group if she changed her mind. The after-school program director is hoping I can talk you into taking on two more boys that go there as well. I explained that your plate is full. Apparently, teenagers in that area are into stealing and starting up gangs. One of the boys said one of the teens showed him a gun. We do what we can. David's mother says you're doing a good job as well.

Eudonis Warner,

Lead Counselor

423 NW 27th Terrace

Ft. Lauderdale, FL 33313

Sunrise Family Services

305-***-****

September 2

> Tiff:
>
> *Know you are excited about your success with David. I am, too. Knew you'd be great with kids. Although you're getting asked to take on other kids, I agree that you should keep it down to just David.*
>
> *4:14 p.m.*

> *I'm sure you do.*
>
> *4:16 p.m.*

> Tiff:
>
> *Lol. What?*
>
> *4:18 p.m.*

> *Yeah. Everybody's just so desperate for any kind of black male to step up that even I seem like a godsend. Remember when I had CPR training for this counseling, I messed up on the dummy, pressing too hard to stimulate breathing? This kid's already had his ribs cracked as it is.*
>
> *4:20 p.m.*

Tiff:

Calm down, Howard. You're so uncomfortable with taking compliments. Can I at least say you're "remarkably decent"?

4:32 p.m.

Lol. How did you know I would be decent at this? This doesn't mean I'll be a perfect father.

4:40 p.m.

Tiff:

Simply because you worry about being decent at it. Sometimes that's all that's needed. I love you. I 'm proud of you. I know a lot about you, not nearly enough, but a lot.

4:51 p.m.

Like what?

4:53 p.m.

Tiff:

Like after dinner when you're in bed typing and start to sigh or tap the side of the laptop with your index finger, you're writing something (on Facebook to ol' professor most likely) from your heart. That the deeper it is the more likely you'll go to bed immediately afterwards. You never tell me what it is you've thought or wrote. I know you get fatherly advice from your ol' professor that you won't ask from your father.

4:56 p.m.

How you know that?

5:01 p.m.

Tiff:

Right after you and professor (Lovitt?) talk on the phone, you call your father with a brand new way of looking at things. It's as if you use Lovitt's fatherly advice to impress your father, as if you came up with the new idea on your own.

5:04 p.m.

It's Lovelett. You have people you talk to.

5:06 p.m.

Tiff:

And you've met them all. I've never met him. I've asked you a million times about when I could meet him. If he's that important to you, he's that important to me to know. Why do you keep me on the outside of you?

5:09 p.m.

I'm sorry. I'm just stupid. I love you. I'm just stupid. I'm just fixing things in my head so that I'm worthy of you.

5:11 p.m.

Tiff:

There you go zig-zagging from swagger to Mr. Pitiful.
Lol. Let me walk with you. Please. Things have gone
pretty easy for us. I know. The untested love I have for
you is restless and more courageous than I would be
on my own. I don't mind going where it takes me.

5:14 p.m.

Love you. You make me a better man.
Gotta work. Just got to David's.

5:18 p.m.

September 2, 2009

Journal:

I've been thinking about how David disses me. If I didn't suck as a human being, I would have set him straight on it by now. It's the story of my life, the reason why I hate coming around here. The guilt has taken me over bit by bit, making me unrecognizable to myself, like the neglect has West Grove.

I got a call during a meeting at work from Sharia that she had moved in her new apartment. I had jeans in the car and a polo, so I changed before I drove there. I played "Funky Nassau" as I drove by vacant lots of weeds and tires, some with lawn chairs and concrete blocks the homeless sat out under weak-looking oak and small palm trees to make the lots into makeshift parks. The song didn't help. All these for sale signs are ridiculous. If someone ever painted over the murals, I believe the old heads that play dominoes at Billy Rolle Park, the big hat-wearing church women in Macedonia Missionary Baptist, the teachers from Carver Middle holding on to houses they can't afford to keep, would all keel over and die. Yes, they'd all be laid out dead under the shade of these clean, unfriendly condos popping up full of people that won't speak. And *that* would finish off Ma and Dad. I just realized this journal is for you two as well.

When I got there, Sharia was busy with relatives helping her arrange her stuff in the apartment. It too is in need of some beige (God awful, lead-based no doubt) paint, new light fixtures and hand rails free of rust. The breeze from the beach just doesn't match what meets the eye.

Boxes were all over the tiny living room. Even the walls inside were beige with filthy light switches here and there. I greeted her relatives. Sharia, sweaty with nostrils flaring and strands of her bronze, wispy hair wet against her forehead, hugged me. Even her sweat it seemed, smelled of beer. She grinned, moaned and mumbled something about me being a "skinny ol', neat lil' man." I patted Sharia on the back, stressing professionalism. Sharia threw her head back and snapped her fingers, exclaiming I needed to "be happy" about her new place and that this was a "celebration," even though she didn't understand how people functioned in this "humidity and bright-ass buildings." I held Sharia by her arms (biceps) to establish distance and stated I was very happy for her. There were at least two interruptions while we talked. Her having gone back and forth from outside to get everything in earlier had drawn several sweaty, gold-toothed dudes to the opened door. Peering in, grinning and licking their lips, both asked if she needed help and if she had a man. She grinned no thanks and pointed at me. The dudes looked at her as if to say, "you sure?" I should have known. Not having anything remotely "'hood" about my clothes and speaking with no slang, it took several responses from her, then me, to get them to move along. They finally did. I was too embarrassed to even address her hinting that I was some sort of boyfriend of hers when their chatter and laughter carried down the hallway.

I asked Sharia if she would reconsider doing the article with the *Gazette*. I emphasized it would be great to show what SFS is doing in the community. Sharia flatly refused, stating that everyone but her and her son would come out of it "looking all grand."   I advised Sharia to take it easy on the alcohol. Sharia talked over my advice, claiming that yes, she knows she "ain't perfect." I assured her I wasn't either. Sharia asked how I was not perfect and would I tell the *Gazette* about such flaws. I again reassured Sharia I "just wasn't" perfect. Sharia shook her head and gently stuck her finger in my chest. She whispered, "Our hurt, we gotta wear it out in the open as it is just so you know us. How 'bout you?"

I remained silent. Sharia regained her composure somewhat and informed me that her apartment was only four doors down from the Effrom boy David continues to fall out with at school and the after-school program. Sharia said she had tried to keep David too busy to go over and attempt to play with Effrom, but Effrom saw him out front unloading belongings from her car and came out. Sharia stated that David was in his room playing Xbox with him. A young woman entered the apartment with a month-old child, an infant that scared the hell out of me. Sharia introduced me to the woman and said the woman was her cousin, Naomi. Naomi noticed I was staring at the child, a dark-skinned, bright-eyed girl. I could feel my shirt starting to stick to my back.

Naomi asked if I wanted to hold the child. I refused and joked that I had enough trouble trying to figure out David as it is. Sharia called David out. He came out, I gave him dap and hugged him in a way that seemed more animated than usual to shield me from looking at this damned little girl. Effrom came behind him.

David told peer that he would see him later. Effrom asked if I was David's "daddy." Sharia snorted. David smirked and insisted that he had already told Effrom that I was "like a play-play uncle or something." Effrom asked if David got his "play-play uncle" because he fights in school. "Naw n****," David snapped, "he our insurance man. Insurance people make him come. It's like insurance on TV." Sharia laughed out loud and danced her way into the kitchen to help with unpacking.

I had to get away from that little girl. I wanted to get out of West Grove. I had David get his basketball. As I took him back out to Virrick Park's court, I suggested he "relax with that n-word business." He snorted and said Effrom "ain't got no daddy" and wanted to come with us and be with him during the session. He said that the "fool" was "actin' all nice" when he came back with a hamburger at the end of the last visit. Effrom asked who had taken him to get it. David shared that he told Effrom his "play uncle" comes around to "hook" him up with "stuff like that all the time so now he wants to be down." I asked what Effrom wanted to be down with. David caught himself from saying his gang, and corrected it by saying people who wanted to be his good friend.

David began to strut onto the court, impervious to the almost violent argument of a nearby couple by a parked car. I informed him of news about gang activity in the area. I warned him to stay away from anyone involved in such a gang. He said he knows already. I instructed him to stop walking on the backs of his shoes and warned him to not become as obnoxious as Effrom. I explained what obnoxious meant as he sighed and fixed his shoes. I also advised him to be nice to his second cousin and her infant daughter. He laughed and claimed that I looked at the woman's infant like the child was "crazy." I assured him that this was not the case and that I just like to be safe around children and infants.

As we played a game of one-on-one basketball, I asked if Sharia drank a lot. David shrugged his shoulders. He then became quite disrespectful. During play he began to dribble and bait me into defending the goal by calling me a "nigga" and a "punk." He told me to "suck on that" when he made a shot. I began to score points and block some of his shots. He began to pout and eventually kicked the ball into the high surrounding fence. His shoe, which had somehow slipped off (most likely from David sliding back onto the back of his shoes again) went flying with the ball. I stated that he better "get it together quickly and bring the ball back." He eventually retrieved ball and shoe. I let him practice his shooting while I explained that I did not intend to make him feel bad when I asked the question about his mother. David stared at me for a moment, dribbling the ball in one place. I emphasized the point and suggested ways in which he could express anger toward Effrom and others through controlled, respectful and direct verbalizations. I suggested he say, "That's personal business." David quickly repeated, "That's personal business." I suggested he tell peers that bother him, "I think it's a good idea if you leave me alone right now." He complained that such a comment was "gay" and would get him laughed at in school. I stated that we would have more talks about how ignorant it was to call everything he disliked "gay."

David said that me saying that sounded "gay" too and insisted the command to get out of his face works for everybody bothering him. I disagreed, reminding him that he still gets in trouble too much for that to truly work. He insisted the problem was "dumb adults" that always take the side of other children against him.

I suggested David approach adults in a more respectful tone and by saying, "excuse me" or "can I talk to you for a minute?" He laughed and said he was finished shooting. I walked him back and - carefully - congratulated him on his basketball skills. (I told him his dribbling was "alright," but that he "better not let it go to his head"). He smiled and said it was "no big deal" (a careful thank you, perhaps), and made a point of trying between the legs dribbling from then on until we reached the car.

Howard Capelton

The mother moved into her apartment. I went over to see the boy and she said something that annoyed me, something to the affect that she can see that I look down on her because of her faults. I don't think I do even though she was drinking and I told her to relax with all that. She said she has to wear her faults, and her hurt out in the open. I guess she has to in order for others to help her, she has to show it. I told her I had troubles too. Either she didn't believe it or implied that I was in some type of life where mine are either allowed to be hidden or merely accepted. I wish that was the only thing that had me thinking while I was there. The mother had a cousin hanging out over there who has a month-old daughter. Dr. Lovelett, I don't think I can do this anymore. The little girl, the newborn. If that didn't put my stuff out in the open, I don't know what else they want. The little girl looks just like her. I don't think I can do this anymore.
Sept. 2

Victor Lovelett

Wait, you said she looks just like her? That's impossible.
Sept. 2

Howard Capelton

Doc, I've kept a picture of her in my wallet since I was in high school. I'm dealing with all this inner-city masculinity confusion in order to reach out. I'm trying to do it all in order to help this kid and make up for everything I did. I know the crease of the picture's top right corner with my eyes closed. I know the faded gold Olan Mills signature, copyright 1984 at the lower right-hand corner.
Sept. 2

Victor Lovelett

What did you do when you saw the child?
Sept. 2

Howard Capelton

I made some small talk I can't even remember. I made some stuff up on the report until I got to when I remembered telling him to get his basketball so we could get out of the house. I had trouble breathing walking to the court. He kept asking me if I was alright. I didn't put all that in the report. If I did, I would start looking crazy.
Sept. 2

Victor Lovelett

Only to those who don't know the full story.

Sept. 2

Howard Capelton

And no one else will! I'm going to do whatever I have to so Tiffany and I can have this damn family life and I can be left alone. If this means ending this, fine by me.

Sept. 2

Victor Lovelett

Stick it out with the boy. This has happened for a reason. You're being challenged to confront your issues, somewhat in a way that the boy's mother spoke of. If you quit this counseling assignment, that little girl's face will appear in some picture on some colleague's desk at work, some baby shower picture on Facebook that you'll keep coming back to. Lessons that aren't learned are always repeated.

Sept. 2

Howard Capelton

I didn't plan on all this. I'm going to make it a rule that I pick him up at the after-school center.

Sept. 2

Victor Lovelett

What about the young ones at the daycare. They didn't bother you?

Sept. 2

Howard Capelton

No little girl there looks like this. The same maple syrup colored skin, the round face, the large, bright eyes. The barely there eyebrows, full head of hair and fat arms. The little

dimple dots on the fists where knuckles should be. I'll wait outside when I go to get him at the after-school place if I need to. I'll honk the horn.
Sept. 2

Victor Lovelett
You don't think this may cause the boy to take this as rejection towards him?
Sept. 2

Howard Capelton
I don't give a damn. I don't care. I'll explain it later. I can't control who they keep in the house. I swear to God if I get through this I will never do another single, solitary thing to anyone ever. If that girl started gurgling or anything I would have clawed my eyes out.
Sept. 2

Victor Lovelett

Howard, the little girl is not your sister. I don't say no struggle, no progress to be dismissive. This is real.

Sept. 2

Victor Lovelett

Howard, what's going on? When's the next time you and the boy meet?

Sept.3

September 4, 2009

Journal:

Sharia greeted me at the door with several spelling papers David had received where he had scored B's. Sharia seemed tired but smiled. I asked who was home. Sharia said her son and herself and asked why. I lied and said I just wanted some peace and quiet while I went over his work and talked with him. As I stood there going over the grades, Sharia hooked me by the crook of my arm and guided me around some unpacked boxes to a corner of the living room. I was preparing to establish distance when she laid a hand on my shoulder and apologized for "any mess" she may have said when I last visited. She joked that she was afraid I would not come back because of it. I assured Sharia that it would take more than that to terminate the sessions.

I congratulated David about his grades as he came from the kitchen. He crunched the lollipop that was in his mouth and swallowed it. We sat at the kitchen table. I asked if making such grades was difficult. David smiled, told me to "just say hard" instead of difficult, and shook his head no, making the grades wasn't "hard." I handed him crayons and clean sheets of paper and challenged him to draw better than me. He accepted, and said he could "do Power Rangers way better" than me and wanted to know who were the people that made the murals of "dancing Bahamians and girls" on the walls of places in West Grove. I said I did not know.

We began drawing. David asked why I was scared of "little babies." I insisted that his relative just took me by surprise. I stated that I had been thinking of getting a dog for a pet, anything to throw him off his line of questioning. I asked if he had ever been in charge of a pet or something of that nature. He said no, but he is in charge of cleaning his room. He grumbled that that wasn't right because his room had to be clean but "boxes and junk everywhere else in here." I said Sharia just wanted him to know where his things are for school. He mumbled that she just wanted to keep him "stuck in the room while she be sleep and stuff."

After discussing the importance of cleanliness, we finished some drawings. He is an incredible artist and was somewhat impressed with my drawing. He said my picture did not look like any Power Ranger though. I let him have the drawing and handed him a ping pong ball. I said the ping pong ball would be his little brother for a few days. He named it Effrom at first. I suggested he choose a different name. He chose Tupac. I instructed him to watch over Tupac at all times, that when he eats, Tupac must eat. That he must not let Tupac fall out of the bed when they go to sleep. David interrupted me, saying he "knows already," that "Child Services will take the child away and he won't get checks and his kid no more."

I instructed David to take Tupac to school but not let him be dropped or handled roughly by anyone. He said he already knew that babies can't be dropped like that so every time Tupac falls and bounces, he'd be dead. I informed him that shaking Tupac was just as dangerous. I shared with him that this experiment will show what it's like for adults who are responsible for children. He cradled Tupac in his hand and remained quiet for a moment, as if truly considering the weight of the responsibility. He said, softly but with wonder, "they shook me and I ain't die."

I stated that such adults disgust me, that hurting children is the worst thing anyone can do. I think my volume surprised him somewhat. He nodded slowly in agreement. "Girls too, unless they real big and fat and trying to fight you anyway." I advised he stay clear of laying his hands on girls at all and asked what he disliked the most about people that have to be in charge. David stated flatly that adults are always "forgettin' stuff or bullyin'." I asked him to give more examples. He said he wanted to do karate, but now karate was just "weird." He stated that he was outside a few days ago "play-fighting" with a peer from the neighborhood and got laughed at when he tried to karate kick peer.

He said his peer and some older boys nearby laughed and told him he "ain't no Bruce Lee." He held Tupac close to his heart and appeared shaken by the fact that the nearby older boys, who probably were around the age of mother's attackers, had criticized him. He said the older boys were the ones that were supposed to be in charge but that they bullied him. I apologized about the boys harassing him. I suggested he tell them he was going to be some kind of "UFC fighter or something."

I shared with David that he would come across a lot of people of all ages who are jealous of him. I explained that jealous people will attempt to make themselves feel better by making him feel bad about what he has, can do or gets to do. I also explained that some people are simply ignorant and don't know any better, and, unfortunately, a lot of ignorant people are older than him. His voice came close to shaking as he said he did not want to have to explain everything he likes to those types of people and that there were too many of them around. I emphasized that this is why boxing and karate are not things to play with because once he uses them, it can cause more trouble than it is supposed to settle. He said he now wanted do boxing. I emphasized both are only for self-defense, not play-fighting and showing off to friends. He asked what he should do if somebody in charge bullies him. I advised him to continue telling other adults until something gets done about it – especially if they touch him inappropriately or anything of that nature. David shyly asked if he could tell me and maybe I could do something sometimes.

I said that's why I was there for David in the first place, to look out for him and see how he's doing. He giggled and punched me in the arm and then exclaimed, "But you so small. You can't fight. You just be joggin'. You must be packin' (meaning carrying a gun)." I told him not to worry about that. He began to eye my shoulder bag as if wondering where the supposed gun was hidden. He said he wanted to be a policeman when he grows up, in fact "half policeman, half John Cena (a professional wrestler)." I asked him why this was so. He studied Tupac and said so he can make people do what's right. He said he would get the boys "who did that" to Sharia and "shoot them in their faces." I struggled with the comment. He clarified that first he would fight them and if they teamed up on him or "banked" him (Richmond slang), he would just shoot them in the face.

I suggested that David assume that all those boys involved went to jail long before he would be a police man. Then, I asked, what he would do as a police man. He said he would "show adults how to be adults for real." He complained that Tupac was making his palms sweaty. I assured him that sweaty palms are only the beginning. He said that my face "got sweaty" when he looked at his second cousin's infant. I praised him for taking on the responsibility of being in charge of Tupac. He accepted the compliment with no fuss. As I ended the session and reached the door, Sharia came close to hugging me. I stepped back to make her shake my hand instead.

Howard Capelton

Still at it. Saw him at their apartment. He got clowned by some older kids for doing some karate moves as opposed to boxing. He got pissed and talked of shooting some of them in the face. I don't blame him. Some deserve to be put out of their misery.
Sept.4

Victor Lovelett

I know what you're doing. Don't let disgust with yourself project onto others.
Sept.4

Howard Capelton

I gave him a ping pong ball to parent to understand responsibility and how hard it is to be an adult. We'll see how it goes.
Sept.4

September 8, 2009

Journal:

I fought insane traffic and nodding off at red lights to reach Fairchild After-School Program with a bag of salt-free corn chips and an apple for David. He greeted me with a mouthful of what I learned was his second Honey Bun since arriving there from school. I instructed him to close his mouth when he chews and took note of how the majority of children at the program were overweight beyond mere "baby fat." He is a bit on the husky side.

I attempted to explain to David that being that heavy can actually take years off of one's life. Unable to talk with the Honey Bun in his mouth, he pointed to himself to show he wasn't overweight. I reminded him of how jittery he gets after eating such things. He grinned, folded his arms and hid his hands in his armpits. I shared that people don't need to be overweight to acquire diabetes. He frowned in confusion. I changed the term diabetes to "high blood sugar" and made him fix his shoes.

I had David me direct me to Mr. Sanford the administrator. He did so and did a flurry of cartwheels as I spoke with Sanford about the amount of sugar being fed to the children and the rate of diabetes in the black community. Sanford agreed about the sugar but stated that the kids refuse to eat fresh fruits, laugh at the granola bars and have to be told to drink water as a punishment. I wanted to say that his job was to make sure David is not a statistic. I said I would look into providing him with a weekly supply of snacks. Sanford applauded the idea but warned that David was hypersensitive to what his peers thought of him and would most likely throw the snacks away and do without rather than be considered different in that regards. I asked how David was handling being "different" as far as me coming to pick him up. Sanford smiled and stated that David enjoys that difference, in fact, he seems aware that practically no other child there is ever picked up by an adult male my age. Sanford said that David now brags to several peers that tend to pick at him by saying that I am his "momma's friend" who "just likes him so much" that I just pick him up to "do stuff " with him.

I caught up with David just as he was getting reprimanded for the excessive cartwheels. I started off to the car with David en route to a community outing. I asked to see Tupac as I drove off. David, sweaty, grimaced, buckled his seat belt and stated that he kept Tupac in his book bag. He said "stuff" in his bag must have moved around too much because Tupac looks "a lil' smooshed so he probably dead." I ran through the list of requirements to take care of Tupac and discovered that he forgot to feed and bathe Tupac. He admitted to getting "bored" with holding Tupac while at the after-school program and asked an assistant there to let Tupac rest high up on a bookshelf. He admitted Tupac was still on the bookshelf. I got in lane to drive back to pick up Tupac while he argued to let Tupac "just sleep for a while." I asked if that's what he hated about a lot of fathers, always leaving their Tupacs with others. I asked if it was difficult to be in charge of someone. David hesitated and said yes. We got Tupac. He was dented up. I went on toward the karate class.

David quickly argued against taking karate as soon as he realized where I was headed. I parked in the karate school parking lot and asked if, deep in his heart, was he as excited as the first time they had come. He mumbled yes. I presented him with a book on karate. He smiled but looked around as if to make sure touching the book was a wise decision. I emphasized that he cannot be a weak follower that gives up who he really is for a bunch of ignorant people.

I explained that most of those people would want David to be a class clown that messes up in school and has no true interests, so that they would always have someone to keep them company at doing nothing with their lives. I explained that if he was like that he would never become a man, a real adult, and would only live to entertain them like a lost puppy. He stated that he was a man and that Sharia said he was the "man of the house." I asked him if men should leave their children asleep on top of bookshelves. I assured him that he would see many "males" making babies with females and thinking that it was cool to never come around to check on the child and teach them how to live. I said real men think for themselves and don't just follow crowds. He hugged the book, lowered his head on its edge and asked what it was like where I lived. I patted him on his shoulder. He closed his eyes as though he were falling asleep from my touch. He asked if I had any babies. My stomach turned. I said no, I was not a father yet. David unbuckled his seat belt and said, "You should be one."

I played some John Coltrane and then went into the dojo (karate school) with David. He peered over the book as the class practiced punches and combinations, switching hands to hold Tupac. He sat up and said kiai under his breath (kiai – the sound karate practitioners make as they hit an object) with every kick and punch the class performed. We sat there for about half an hour before I said it was time to go. He complained that they had just gotten there. I baited him, stating that there was not a good reason for him to see the "other cool stuff" that the class was about to do because it would really make him want to join the class and, of course, he could not do what he wants because of where he lives. He grinned at Tupac, as if to say, "This apple think he slick."

I drove him to the Books-A-Million bookstore. David stated that he heard the instructor say the word honor in the class. He reminded me that I was supposed to tell him what honor meant. I said honor means a person has enough self-respect that they would never allow themselves do ridiculous things. He said "maybe boxers got honor, too." I said told David he would still practice meditating. He said he could not because "no boxer does that stuff, they just punch." I explained that meditating was more important for him than boxing or karate because he needed to find ways to settle his mind because it would help him do better in school and keep his tantrums in check. I said getting jumpy from too much sugar makes it much harder to meditate and focus. I assured him that if his behavior and grades did not continue to improve, he would not be able to do either anyway because boxing and karate are rewards for doing well in school and at home.

I suggested a way he could do better in school and home was by using magic words like "sir" and "ma'am" when asking for things or responding to adults. David thought for a moment and then complained that such words were some "army mess" and that he "ain't in no army." I suggested he try it for a day and see what happens. David stared at me as I drove him back to after-school program. I asked him what was wrong. He shook his head, smiled and said that he "didn't know," that I "was just weird" the way I "know stuff." He looked at the dented, dirty Tupac ping pong ball in his hand. He said some boys on his bus were "messing" with him about watching Tupac. He asked if my friends mess with me about seeing him. I said no, but if they did, I would tell them to get out of my face. I told him that adults are not perfect, but that they try their best to do what's right – and that, yes, some can try harder. I took the ping pong ball, thanked him for "trying to be a good adult" and ended our session. David whispered "yes sir" and hurried inside.

Howard Capelton

You called him DAP man, as in slapping him five, giving him dap.

Sept.8

Victor Lovelett

I sit on an advisory board for the National Association for the Education of Young Children. Our position statement was actually called Developmentally Appropriate Practice in Early Childhood Programs, or DAP, for short.

Sept.8

Howard Capelton

The notes I have to write to my supervisor about the sessions with him are called DAP notes.

(D) Description (A) Assessment (P) Plan: I give an assessment of data gathered and state what I'll try for the next session.

I guess we can call him Lil DAP then. Had a talk with the administrator at the after-school program. The man damn near had every excuse in the world for why I shouldn't bother with trying to get some decent food for Lil DAP to eat while he is there. I wish I could bring him the health specs we use at work to determine whether we'll cover people with life insurance. You can exercise and pay more for healthy food and have less medication and sickness in the long run or eat trash up front and have legs amputated from diabetes later. Must every social menace require a gun pointed sideways at them for them to get the picture?

Sept.8

Victor Lovelett

Even then, some would become immune to it.

Sept.8

Howard Capelton

Lil DAP most likely killed lil Tupac the ping pong ball. He said he put Tupac in his book bag and things shifted around in it and dented Tupac up. Lol. I discovered Tupac was not fed or bathed either. Maybe Lil DAP will give adults more of a break the next time he thinks of judging us.

Sept.8

Victor Lovelett

We do the best we can, don't we?

Sept.8

Howard Capelton

We discussed the word honor. This boy told me words like sir and ma'am were army words. He told me I should be a father.

Sept.8

Victor Lovelett

Smart kid

Sept.8

September 9

> Tiff:
>
> Just reminding you that I will be home late after Yolanda's baby shower. You can come by if you want. Lol
>
> 11:13 a.m.

> What do you think us having a baby will do for us?
>
> 11:15 a.m.

> Tiff:
>
> You know, to fulfill a dream I've always had of being a mother. Also to bring about something that will allow you to finally share more of yourself with me — more of your hopes, your fears, and, if not with me, then at least with something or someone I had a part in creating.
>
> 11:17 a.m.

Tiff:

I love you.

I love us.

11:23 a.m.

September 9, 2009

Journal:

I'm going to apologize for the way this entry winds up sounding at the end. Tiffany, Ma and Dad, you will understand everything when all of this is all over.

I drove to Sharia's half asleep. I would do anything for a solid night's sleep. Anyway, she was out front talking to neighbors and greeted me with news of her landing a job at a local gas station/convenient store off Dixie Highway. Sharia had a beer in her hand and warned me not to start that "A program (AA – Alcoholics Anonymous) @*^* (stuff) today." Sharia said she had taken out the beer for me because she knew I was coming. I declined. Sharia's voice was loud like the last time I saw her intoxicated when she first moved in. Sharia's eyes were somewhat hazy. As I walked up, she got in front of me and danced even though there was no music. Sharia hollered for David to come outside while still dancing. I gave Sharia a long, hard look. Sharia rolled he eyes and grumbled that she bet my woman "cain't do a damn thing" around me. The neighbors, older women, laughed. I stared at her, then the bottle. She hurled the full bottle of beer down to the sidewalk. It burst along the curb. Sharia threw her hands up and stated, "How bad can I be if I got me a job, huh?" Sharia joked that she could now get all the unhealthy food she wanted.

I yawned and asked how she and David were getting along. Sharia said that he had punched the side of the refrigerator and hurt his hand because his father was supposed to call and see how he was doing. She said he had kept his hand in a jar of ice water and huffed on and on about that although I was "all small," I probably had a gun and "might shoot anybody in they face" that messed with him. I expressed concern for how violent he was with his descriptions. I couldn't bring myself to mention some of the pictures he drew. Sharia shrugged her shoulders and muttered, "He nine years-old. He a boy." Sharia stated she was about to go in the kitchen. I assured Sharia that I was unarmed and that being a boy should not require such graphic statements. Sharia shared that the more David's father lets him down, the more David expects me to "look out for" him, and possibly, for her as well.

I asked to speak with David alone for a minute. I walked in, leaving Sharia outside with neighbors. The scent of Egyptian musk incense hit me as I greeted him. He sat on a black, crème and beige floor rug in front of a cracked, black pleather couch watching an outdated flat screen TV that sat on a modest stereo system. He kept his right hand in a Mason jar of iced water. The apartment was starting to have some order to it. The boxes were gone. Pictures of Sharia posing in a champagne glass setting hung over the TV. It reminded me of a ghetto mall I came across in North Miami for a wrongful death claim. A picture of David and Sharia sat on the glass living room table, next to one of Naomi and that child. *Sister2Sister* magazines and coasters made of cork filled out the rest of table. A vase here and there made it clear this was a woman's house. Other than that, no reading material was in sight. I turned the TV off and talked with David about school. He informed me that I "don't have to turn the TV off to talk." I checked his swollen hand to make sure nothing was broken. It wasn't too bad. I explained there's a difference between having someone's attention and having someone's full attention. I said I wanted his full attention. I asked how he hurt his hand. He stated that he was sure his mother already told me because she "always talkin' 'bout what I do." I tried to change his mood. I asked if he had a girlfriend at school. David grinned and said he didn't know yet because the girl likes another boy, as well.

I praised David for taking his time to get to know the girl. I said he should take his time to get to know people like his Sharia does. I gave an example of how his Sharia does not let any random guy that smiles at her into their house. David stated that she does let this one man in that he did not like. He said she met him at Mr. Walt's barbershop, where she takes David to get haircuts. He said he does not say anything to the man and the man does not say anything to him. I worked with him on meditation exercise to improve his focus and attention span. He squirmed and grew impatient with the sounds of Sharia's loud laughter and cursing with neighbors just beyond the front door. I told him that doing exercises will aid him in lessening the negative reactions he experiences when dealing with peers and adults from time to time. He snapped his fingers and stated that this was like he was giving himself a "time out" in his head. I agreed and suggested he try breathing and counting ten deep breaths to help him during irritating situations.

David's second cousin Naomi came in with that baby. I focused on my own breathing. He picked the infant out of stroller as Naomi greeted us. I warned him to be careful with picking up infants. I reminded him of the shape Tupac the ping pong ball was in these days. Naomi said it was alright for him to pick up the child. They both laughed at me, noting that I appeared to be holding my breath as he held the little girl. He brought her to me. I quickly thanked him, and refused. Naomi and David insisted. I again refused and told him to stop fooling around. He asked why men "always hate kids like that." He reminded me that he had to hold Tupac the ping pong ball or "at least try it" when he didn't want to. I held the infant. My skin crawled. Naomi laughed and told me to breathe. Sharia came in and laughed, too. I demanded Sharia not laugh so loudly or else she would startle the infant. Sharia joked that I looked constipated. I handed the infant over to Naomi and informed them that the baby looked like someone I knew and if that was a problem then perhaps she could discuss it with my supervisor.

It was a little excessive. I know. Sharia and David were stunned. Sharia asked why was I "actin' all like that." I wiped my face and said what I did with him was a job in itself and should be respected as such. I hopped over boxes to the bathroom and vomited. Sharia checked on me and offered a beer. I objected. She said she did not have any ginger ale and beer "fizzed up" just the same. I refused and lied that I had been feeling under the weather all day. "No," Sharia whispered, "you look tired. Somethin's eatin' you up." Really? You think? Sharia asked what it was. I assured her I was fine. She needed to mind her business.

I sat with David and apologized for the outburst. He asked if I was okay. I nodded and arranged a behavioral contract where he agreed to not "go off" on people as much and in doing so, I would continue to do cool stuff with him like play basketball. It was a godsend. I needed something to make me feel like the adult again, that I was in control and that did it. He informed me that my hands were shaking, and asked if I wanted to "go be quiet and breathe" in his room. I balled my fists, thanked David for the suggestion, declined, and ended our session.

Chapter 4 – Fakin' It

Howard Capelton

They made me hold her. The baby. She looks just like Karen. She smells like her.

Sept.9

Victor Lovelett

All babies smell like that! That girl is not your younger sister!

Sept.9

Howard Capelton

I know spirits can return into newborns. An elder dies and a young one is born with the same features, same expressions. You haven't read so many things that you've forgotten that. I know, I held her. She frowned and got quiet like she recognized me from somewhere.

Sept.9

Victor Lovelett

You were just there the other day. The child most likely doesn't hear too many deep male voices.

Sept.9

Howard Capelton

I gave the kid back and threw up in their bathroom. I told them I ate something and was feeling bad, but the drunk ass mother's all in my face saying, no something's eating you up. Like something's bothering me. They're on to me.

Sept.9

Victor Lovelett

Who? The mother and child?

Sept.9

Howard Capelton

And the cousin, the little girl. Everyone.

Sept.9

Victor Lovelett

You got through it. Perhaps the more you see her, the less of a reaction it will be. Imagine if you were able to be there for Lil DAP and grow to care for the infant girl?

Sept.9

Howard Capelton

Serves me right. She'll torture me the whole time I'm dealing with this boy. They got so little but so much going on.

Sept.9

Victor Lovelett

You can't demand Lil DAP and his mother grow beyond their comfort zones while you sit back totally content within yours. Get a beer or two and call me later, if you need to.

Sept.9

Howard Capelton

Didn't go into work today. Head is all screwed up. Getting my mind ready to meet him later on today. Drank three beers when I got home.

Sept.10

Victor Lovelett

I said two, man! Lol You okay? I'm standing in the hall messaging you while my class takes an exam. A student passing by just chastised me since I'm always on them about their phones in class.

Sept. 10

Howard Capelton

Still thinking about meeting Lil DAP. Forgot to say that yesterday, before the baby thing started, the mother was out in front of her apartment drinking. She found herself a gas station attendant job. I don't know how she'll manage with all that beer and liquor around. Lil DAP's father was supposed to call him but didn't. The kid punched the refrigerator. He told her that, since I'm small, I must have a gun and will shoot anyone that bothers me, him or his mother. She said the more his father lets him down, the more he's expecting me to be ready to look out for him and his mother – by any means necessary.

Sept. 10

Victor Lovelett

At least you know he's accepted you. Remember when you were unsure if he would even respect you?

Sept. 10

Howard Capelton

The mother blew his gun talk off around her and that baby as a boy being a boy. She practically said a boy has to be willing to get violent in order to – never mind. He has to stand up for himself sure but, I don't know.

Sept. 10

Victor Lovelett

You want him to whoop ass so people will leave him alone, but you don't want him doing drive by's into crowds either.

Sept. 10

Howard Capelton

If something goes wrong when I get over there, I'm calling you.

Sept.10

September 10, 2009

Journal:

I drove to David's after-school program to pick him up. One of the assistants informed me that he was in a room by himself because he had gotten into a scuffle with Effrom. I sat with him and asked what had happened. He said Effrom was calling him a "nerdy fag" all day because he mentioned that I was coming to get him earlier that day. Effrom had laughed at David, saying he acted like I'm his boyfriend and that I "ain't real (meaning macho, or street-oriented) anyway."

David said he told Effrom to get out of his face. Effrom proceeded to call me "nerdy fag" and said I picked up him so we could "get each other in the butthole." David said he told the afterschool van driver to get Effrom away from him, but driver didn't listen. He said the teasing escalated as they got into the building and he retaliated by saying Effrom was just mad because he didn't have a daddy. Effrom pushed him down and David hit him in the face with the big attendance book people sign to get their kids. I went over to the assistant to ask if David had informed van driver of Effrom antagonizing him. The assistant said driver was told but that they were going down the road and were within several blocks of Fairchild after-school program facility.

The assistant confirmed that Effrom did get physical first and was to receive more punishment but David snatched his arm from assistant's grasp and began kicking chairs and screaming. I brought David over to hear assistant's account of the incident. I praised him for having spoken to an adult about the situation beforehand and refraining from being the first to get physical when things escalated. I assured assistant that I would work on his response after the scuffle. As I drove him to Books-A-Million bookstore, he was quiet and seemed to watch me for any sudden movement. He buckled his seat belt and pulled the backs of his shoes up on the sly and asked, "You gone keep picking me up then?" I stated yes and explained that I did not expect him to change his response to certain situations overnight. I explained that the consequence to the overreaction would be him writing a letter to the assistant, but that I did recognize that he showed progress by warning the assistant beforehand.

I stated that this was all a process in helping him decrease disruptive and negative attention seeking behaviors and develop positive social skills. David asked what process meant. I said process means a slow change. He asked if I was in a process. I said I was trying to be in one. He brought up the last time I visited his house and asked if things I said during the visit were a process. I nodded and said I was trying to change into being a better person, and that I did not mean to talk like I was ready to stop seeing him.

We arrived at Books-A-Million. I explored perceived pay-offs of getting angry about certain situations compared to more constructive means to deal with disappointments. David stated that people have to get mad sometimes so people will stop messing with them. His said it was "too hard to be okay when ni- (stops and catches himself) *apples* be in yo' face like that." He asked what smart people do when they get mad. I emphasized that he was smart. I said smart people can lose their cool like he did, it's just that there is hope that the more intelligent a person is, the less embarrassing and self-destructive their blow ups become. This knucklehead asked what do I do when I "really really get mad." I said I might curse. He asked if I cursed "for real" or if I say "flinkin' flankety flarn like white people."

I laughed and assured David that I knew how to do it both ways. I stated that his mother said his father has a temper. His face seemed to drain itself of any emotion. I stated that his father was most likely full of rage during childhood because his father was not present in his life. I asked if he was angry because his father was not around either. David looked away, shrugged his shoulders and asked for a candy bar from the café.

I bought David a candy bar. I pulled out a homemade sandwich as David ate. After a few bites, he stated that his father just "works a lot right now" but grew even more sullen and withdrawn. I said I fully understood if he was upset about it but that he could not let it ruin his life at home and time at school. He asked if my father was around when I was his age. I said yes, but not enough. He asked was it because my father's phone was messed up (Sharia shared that this was the excuse she had used to explain father's not being in touch). I said it was most likely because my father did not know how to interact with his family. I assured him that his father not being around had nothing to do with him, that he is a great kid. He exhaled heavily and began to rock in his chair. It seemed as though he struggled to speak for a moment. He began to eat the rest of his candy bar as though it had lost its taste. Instead of pressuring him to talk, I helped with the spelling on his apology letter to the afterschool assistant he said he "hated." We started to leave. I played some Miles Davis. I could hear him humming to try and follow Davis' trumpet. I arrived at after-school program and thanked him for being attentive. He put his hand out for me to give him dap. I "dapped" David "up" and said I would see him tomorrow.

September 11, 2009

Journal:

I drove to David's. I greeted him as he sat at the kitchen table eating a jumbo pack of M&M's and writing a letter. He barely acknowledged me at first, then said that this was the day "those people died in them buildings." I asked what he was doing. He said he was writing a letter to his daddy, and that he got the idea from me making him write the letter to that "dumb lady at after-school." He asked me to check his spelling. I noticed he had included the word "ser." I instructed him in the proper spelling (sir).

I read that David was doing okay and wanted to know if father's phone was still "messed up." He misspelled my name when he stated that I was "smart and good" and that his father should come and see him so people will say they look alike. I said that there were magic words he could use that could help him get what he wanted from adults. I quickly said that they were not guaranteed, but that I have had a lot of success with them. I said two of those words are "please" and "thank you."

David complained that such words sounded like "slavery." He said that it sounded like things people have to say when teachers make them or if they're begging or "fakin' like they nice to get somethin'." He said if he started saying that to kids "for no reason" (meaning if no adult was around to make him), he would be called a punk. I said to practice it only near adults in the meantime. I reminded him that I used the words and was just as much a man as anyone else. David reminded me that I was "old already."

I informed David that there are things that are important regardless of one's age. I presented him with a book called "*Whoopi's Big Book of Manners*." We read over it, which discussed cleaning up after oneself, manners for the movie theatre (meaning stop talking during the movie!), even specific manners for adults. He enjoyed the idea of special manners for adults, teasing me for needing to learn "extra." I then presented him with a children's book called *"How to Take the Grrrr out of Anger."* We went over the book's list of the body's anger "warning signs," six steps to solving anger problems and various ways to calm down. He was again surprised and entertained, particularly that there were so many people of color in the book. I then worked with him on his meditating exercises. He counted his breaths up to twelve before having to start over and also had difficulty keeping his eyes closed. His voice even sounded more relaxed after meditation. He asked when he would do karate. I asked what about boxing. He smiled and stated that he figured karate was "already boxing with your hands plus you kick people in they face if you feel like it, too." I said I would talk to Sharia about it, who I could see was outside talking with neighbors. I told him he was an excellent reader and ended session.

Howard Capelton

What his mother said about Lil DAP is appearing to come true. He's listening to me more now that his father's not talking with him. He tried to resolve a conflict the exact way I suggested and, just as he said to me several times, it would not work. Some punk at the after-school program (actually the same boy he lives next to and plays with), called me a fag for always picking Lil DAP up. Lil DAP told them about it when the boy kept up and they did nothing – until he hit the kid in the face with a book. He was scared that I would get so mad I wouldn't come to see him anymore.

Sept.12

Victor Lovelett

You see, that's how valuable you are to him. That's how valuable you'll be to your own children as well.

Sept.12

Howard Capelton

Slow down, doc. Lol. I actually started calling him Lil DAP. He says it's cool. I'm working on him not using the word nigga. He's devised a substitute – apples.

Sept.12

Victor Lovelett

Sounds like you two have developed your own little world.

Sept.12

Howard Capelton

This knucklehead said he didn't believe I could really get mad or that I curse. He said he thought I'd curse like white people (flinkety filth flam, like Yosemite Sam or something)

Sept.12

Victor Lovelett

Lol! Boy do I wish I could meet this kid.
Sept.12

Howard Capelton

He's taken to writing letters to his dad, since the guy won't call. He's using the stupid army words like "sir" in the letters. It's mind-blowing. He stopped at using words like "please." He said those sound like "slavery words." His philosophy on that was enlightening. He's also decided to pursue karate – in spite of the neighborhood boys clowning him for it.
Sept.12

Victor Lovelett

He's deciding to be his own person beyond the dictates of his environment. That means your influence is outshining the neighborhood as well!
Sept. 13

September 14, 2009

Journal:

After stopping by the old house, then the cemetery, I drove to David's. He greeted me at the door, asking if I was taking him to the karate today. I demanded he pull the heels of his shoes from under his feet first. He pumped his ashy fist, and hissed "Yes!" I got him buckled in and as he complained of my backseat being full of "insurance paper mess," I went over the manners emphasized in the "*Whoopi's Big Book of Manners*" book we read during the previous session. I emphasized that the karate school was an important place to start decreasing bad behaviors and getting along with people. I explained that doing so will keep the karate instructor from making him do lots of push-ups while everybody else will be doing kicks and punches. He boasted that push-ups were easy anyway. I reiterated the importance of his behavior and that I would be watching his every move.

David seemed pleased with hearing I would be paying attention and said, "Yes sir." He said Sharia had been "all nice" since she mailed off his letter to his father. I asked why. He said she read the letter after I left and, that he just guessed she "liked it too much" (Sharia had texted I earlier to say that he had added a "please see me" at the letter's end – with the book I left opened to a page showing the word. Sharia said it made her throat and head hurt all night). He recounted his day at school, saying that he has a girlfriend "for real now." I asked how he knew this. He said that boys and girls who "go together" eat food from each other's plates at lunch time sometimes. He said his new girlfriend let him have her tater tots so he stole the boy's jello that sat next to him and gave it to her. When asked why he didn't give his own jello to her, he said he was hungry because he missed the school breakfast. I asked if Sharia ever made him breakfast. He said not really.

I insisted he not steal. David stated that his girlfriend kissed him by the water fountain "when nobody was looking." He said his girlfriend wore glasses but had a "nice, fat butt like a grown lady." I thanked him for, perhaps, too much information and emphasized that his new books on improving social skills will help with having girlfriends. David asked if I had a girlfriend. I said I was married. He asked if I had babies. I said no and reminded him that he had asked this question before. He countered and said he had asked weeks ago and that maybe I had one now. I sensed him becoming unnerved. He joked that my not having kids was okay since I "act all scary" holding babies anyway. David was quiet for some time afterwards, before stating, "Good, you got a girl. I got one and I'm just nine... and I ain't even got no money." I parked in the karate school's parking lot and showed him a picture of my wife. David commented with surprise that my wife was not light-skinned but "all chocolatey." David quickly patted me on the shoulder and said it was okay because she was pretty enough and that he was willing to bet that she was smart. Satisfied, he then mentioned that he had never seen a "regular dude" as old as I was that didn't have "some kinda baby." I said I was focusing on my career and was looking into having a family in the future.

David joined in with the karate class and, as expected, ran afoul of the instructor's rules concerning talking and playing around. He did several sets of push-ups. He pouted, cried and tried to stomp off to the door. He was sent off to the side to work with a senior student and was reprimanded throughout the course of the class. By the middle of the class, he was in step, punching and kicking the combinations assigned to him. The instructor praised him for several crisp side kicks. He tried to keep a stone face but blushed. After class, I discussed with him more constructive means to deal with disappointments. He realized getting upset in karate class did him no good, in fact, it took away from his time to learn more kicks and punches. I advised him to count to fifteen when he feels himself getting upset, similar to the way he meditates (counting each breath) with me.

I asked him what would happen if the karate instructor let all of his students talk and goof around like he did. He said the class would be crazy "like the bus at school." I agreed and asked if it made sense that instructor kept students from "tripping." He said it made sense. I suggested he look at how the person he is getting mad at has to deal with things sometimes. I asked if he thought his father did such things when he got mad. David said he did not know but said he would ask his father the next time he talked to him or wrote him.

I asked if David's father had responded from his last letter. His face tightened. Annoyed, he blurted out that he already told me how his father "work a lot." I admitted that I understood if he got upset about his father being so busy. He asked me if he thinks about what his father has to do, counts to fifteen and still gets mad, then what? I shared that he had Sharia, relatives and myself to talk to. I assured him talking out such anger with people he trusts is the best way to go. I dropped him off back at the apartment, commented to him and Sharia that he learned a lot in karate class, and has the makings of a great martial artist, and ended the session.

September 16, 2009

Journal:

When I got to David's after-school program, I had to wake him up. He was napping on the floor in front of the TV (the group was watching *Pee-Wee Herman's Adventure*, a classic in my book). He said that everything at school was "pretty straight." He talked about the male visitor that continues to visit Sharia. He said his name was Roman.

I asked if he and Roman got along. He mumbled something under his breath and asked if I wanted to trade my wife for Sharia. That way, he reasoned, I would be his mother's boyfriend and I would "always be here to do stuff" so I won't have to drive back and forth all the time.

As I walked David to the car, he said Roman even hangs out around the house when Sharia is not there. I asked if Roman drank as much as Sharia. David said not as much. I asked if her old boyfriend back in Richmond drank a lot. He said no, but that he "got weed'." He said that Roman did threaten him to "keep quiet" or he would put his "head through the wall." I asked if that was all Roman did. He hesitated and said yes, emphasizing that if I said anything to Sharia, Roman might find out. David appeared stressed as he complained that he hated all men except me and his daddy. I started up the car and considered his aversion to young adult males and older men. He asked why Sharia always "gotta have dumb men around," that they left Richmond to get away from some and now she was bringing more around again. I said women like men the way David's girlfriend likes him. He sank in the chair and grumbled that just "when things get good she always finds somebody that keep it bad."

I had David buckle up. I told him to call next time he felt uncomfortable with Roman. Don't ask me why I did this. He asked me what I would do. I (honestly) said I did not know yet. As I drove to the Books-A-Million bookstore I stressed that he use his "magic words" as we approached the café. He called the cashier "ma'am," said please when he asked for a candy bar and Mountain Dew. He grumbled "thank you" when I switched the candy bar and Mountain Dew to an apple, a bag of chips and cranberry juice. The cashier complimented David on his manners and said I should be proud of my son. He quickly thanked the cashier, as if to keep me from replying. I felt that way down in my soul. I figured now, maybe, I won't go to hell when I die. Maybe. I felt in control. Needed. Competent. He didn't seem so strong anymore. For the first and only time in all of this, I was thankful this Roman showed up in his life. God forgive me. I took him to the children's section of the store. While I took out a sandwich from home, I had David search for a book. He picked a DC Super Heroes book.

I read the book to David and acted confused with certain words so he would help pronounce them. He had difficulty remaining still even though the book was fairly short. He pestered me with why I always brought sandwiches instead of buying one when they came to the bookstore. I informed him that the store did not have BLT sandwiches. I suggested he meditate. He said he would not do "that karate junk in no store" with people around. I suggested ten pushups instead. He said I was crazy. All I know is I was thinking about this Roman that I finished the sandwich, got to the floor and did twenty-five sloppy pushups. He giggled and did seventeen of his own. I had him breathe deeply afterwards (tricking him into meditating). I reiterated how favorably his interactions at the store had been when he used magic words. He said it would not work so well at his school or where he lived because they aren't "magic places" like the bookstore or where I must live. He said he wants to live where I live, where he bets it is "magic all the time."

I assured David that there is no place that's magical all the time. He countered and said Disney World. I said maybe, but offered that he could get a better response if he did not use magic words at school or home when he is already in trouble because it will make people think he is being "fake." I insisted he use them beforehand and things would be a lot smoother for him. I said to use magic words three times at school or home by the next session so I can see what happens. He said magic words do not work, that he used some in his letter to his father and that his father still has not called him. My jaw went a little tight. Oh yeah, I thought, his father. David said he would ask Sharia to please make Roman go away and if she does not then magic words don't work "for real." I bought him a wristband to remind him to use the words more often and see what happens. I drove him home and ended session by giving him dap. Roman wasn't there. I told David he did a good job with keeping the back of his shoes up, as well as his manners and push-ups. He smiled weakly and sighed as he closed the door.

Howard Capelton

The mother has some dude over there she's messing with. Lil DAP and this guy are not getting along either. He even suggested I trade my wife for his mother so things would be easier. I'm working my way through the 'hood politics, trying not to have a nervous breakdown around his infant baby cousin and now some nigga's laid up in the house threatening the kid. Every time I think I'm getting a handle on things, here comes something else.

Sept. 17

Victor Lovelett

Easy, Poppa Howard. Nigga? Don't you mean apples? Lol! Sons are naturally protective of their mothers, especially mothers that have been through what she has been through.

Sept. 17

Howard Capelton

He wasn't like that with me. He was a little suspicious, but this is different. This fool sounds outright abusive.

Sept. 17

Victor Lovelett

You didn't come into this looking to get as involved with his mother as with him. This guy is coming in specifically to be with the mother, right after she suffered an assault, which she or Lil DAP has yet to fully heal from.

Sept. 17

Howard Capelton

But he's depending on me to protect them. Possibly to protect his mother from herself. He said every time things go well, she always hooks up with some tired stereotype that ruins things. She's looking to entertain any low-life so long that keeps her company.

Sept. 17

Victor Lovelett

Be careful with that. Call me and let's discuss ways in which this can be approached.

Sept. 17

September 18, 2009

Journal:

I received call from Sharia earlier, who stated that she had picked up David early from after-school center because he had "acted a fool again." He was reported to have been hit in the head with a ball while playing with others. After not being satisfied with how the adult in charge punished the offending child, he grew enraged and tried several times to kick ball-throwing peer. I stopped by the after-school program. Assistant stated that David then began screaming at a parent and the assistant that he "hated all of them."

Mr. Sanford said he suggested to Sharia that sudden behavior shifts might hint that David needed to be medicated. Sharia insisted that this was not needed. Sanford suggested that the after-school program may not be the best place for him. I told Sanford that David had been working on being more respectful to adults with manners and the like to get adults to see things from his perspective. Sanford had nothing to say.

I drove to the apartment. Sharia answered door in a T-shirt with no bra and the smell of alcohol on her breath. She let me know that she was "aggravated and had company," if that was alright with me. Sharia walked to her bedroom, pointing me to David's room. I found him balled up in a fetal position on his bed, clutching his basketball as if it were a puppy he was hoping to keep. The room was in worse shape than I imagined and I loved it, more confirmation of him needing me.

His small room was a mess and had the lingering scent of clothes in need of a wash. Schoolwork, pennies and gummy bear wrappers were every which way on the floor. The SpongeBob Squarepants sheets on the bed were so unsettled the loud, multi-colored flowers from the dingy mattress and box spring nauseated me. Underneath the bare, sliding window, next to a blue dresser with a busted drawer, stood a plastic GI Joe samurai sword in the corner. It leaned against the wall, like a broom. 3D glasses from a movie theatre sat atop a pile of old shoes and clothes in the closet like a margarita's maraschino cherry. I noticed he had put my drawing of a Power Ranger over his bed with masking tape. I told him I had just come from the after-school program to tell them things we had been working on in order to get along better with everyone. I said an assistant did say he did remember him saying "please" for more snacks and that she did give him a second Capri Sun because of it.

I noticed the picture of David and what had to be his father on the wall by the door. They were sitting on a stoop somewhere. I never knew he could smile like that. I asked him to recount what happened. David said he used the magic words "at" his teacher and that everything was "okay" until two of his peers started to tease him about saying please and thank you when he got his snack at the after-school program. He said the two peers, boys, started blowing kisses at him. He had told one of the staff, who reprimanded them. He began to get upset as he said the boys "kept on doing it" when he was playing tetherball, jumping in between him and a playmate he was playing with and knocking the ball back at him. He said the ball hit him in the mouth and he started chasing them. He said one of the peer's grandmothers came to pick him up just as he lost his shoe from trying to put his "foot in his back and kick." He came close to hyperventilating when he said kids started laughing because his shoe came off. David said the boy's grandmother started yelling at him and he yelled back.

Someone, an adult, walked down the hall by David's window. The window had a frosted finish, allowing only the darkened outline of the person to show. I asked who was the staff member that he said "please" to. He said the "fat lady that breathes hard a lot." I asked if that was the same person that he talked to about the boys. He said yes and that she "got in they faces to stop." I asked if she was the same person watching the kids when he was playing tetherball. He said no. He screamed that Sharia came to get him and "just started yellin' and pullin'" his shirt, which was stretched at the collar. I called Sharia into the room and called Sanford over the phone. Sharia came in still wearing a T-shirt and no bra. She leaned against the door frame. I asked Sanford to contact the staff member that had heard David's being mannerly and asking for intervention regarding the two boys harassing him. I asked Sanford to check David's claims with staff member and call back. That's when things got really stressful.

Roman, a stocky, light-skinned man between mid-twenties to mid-thirties, came from Sharia's bedroom into the room's doorway. He was shirtless with boxers and shorts hanging low off of his behind. Sharia attempted to block his entrance into the room. He pushed her aside and asked who I was. I explained my business there and asked Roman was he the individual who told David he would put his "head through the wall." Roman asked if I wanted my head in a wall next to David. As Roman began to hurl threats, Sanford called back. Sharia argued with Roman as Sanford stated that David was being truthful. I reminded Sanford of David's attempts to be more mannerly. I explained that David had warned me that he would be teased and harassed for doing so, but that I had no idea things would get so out of hand. Sanford admitted that the suggestion for him to be medicated and find somewhere else other than the after-school program was a bit hasty. I got David on the phone, away from Sharia and Roman's fussing. Sanford spoke with him, calmed him down somewhat. Sharia pushed Roman out into hallway and then got onto the phone to speak with Sanford. As Sharia got off phone, Roman came back into the room to grab her by the back of her neck to take her back into her bedroom. I wanted to get up and say something, but I thought, hey, she's the one that brought this fool into all this. He didn't come with the apartment.

Sharia went with Roman. I called out to Sharia to see if she wanted to say anything to David. Sharia came back to the room and struggled to apologize to David, insisting afterwards that his reactions to situations don't help. Roman returned, demanded Sharia go to her bedroom and slammed the door shut. Sharia told us she would be back. As Sharia and Roman argued elsewhere, David told me that that was the Roman he told me about. I told him he knows more than I gave him credit for. I reminded him of recognizing the danger of meditating at the beach and how he knew people would bug him about the magic words. David stared at the drawing over his bed and muttered that he always had to do the hard things, and I just "sit there like other adults, just talking about it." He said the magic words "don't work good" for him because his daddy has not called him. He asked to spend the night at my house. It hurt my heart. I wanted to be needed, but not this much. I said that was not possible. David took off the wristband I bought, threw it across the room and complained that nothing works for him.

David said he wanted to see me do something hard, something that "don't work but people make you keep doin' anyway." He stated that he wanted me to hold his infant second cousin "'til you get sweaty," or lift weights or box or do karate. This is where I knew there was no turning back.

I blurted out that my young sister died as an infant of SIDS (Sudden Infant Death Syndrome). I informed David that this happened when I was very young and that she's in a cemetery not far from the apartment. He asked if my sister was the only one that had SIDS. I explained that my sister and I were the only children. He asked why my mother didn't "have more babies." I explained that she had been ill and had to have an operation that made her unable to have more children, which made me the only child after my sister passed away. He asked what was SIDS and how did it kill my sister. I explained what SIDS was to him. He said that was messed up and wished he had SIDS. I asked why. David said so he could "wake up somewhere like wherever" I "must live." He shivered and mashed his palms into his eyes as if trying to shove his tears back into his skull. I stated that I understood his problem with his father, but assured him that no one's life was easy.

I said that my father likes me well enough and would probably like me less if he knew some of the things I had done as a kid. I told David I would "box or something" soon enough – just for him. I said I understood if he did not want to wear the wristband, but reminded him that the magic words did work and that his peers were probably jealous of him because he was being cool with the adults. He had stopped crying by this point and muttered that he would kick the peer "'til he bleed" next time. I admitted that I would have been mad too and that the peer's grandmother showing up at that point was just bad luck. I reminded him that he must respond with the same amount of force that someone offends him with or else everyone will turn against his wishes. I said I would have hit peer back with the ball. I reminded him that he would see many young boys like him ruin their lives trying to please some fool in the street that couldn't care less about them. I warned that blind anger is usually the way most boys get caught up in trouble they did not plan on having.

I asked David to start thinking about when he got "extra mad" about different things. I said a lot of people get mad in order to not deal with something else. I suggested the avoided topic could be anything from having a headache to missing one's father. I meditated with him until, exhausted, he leaned on my arm. I took him to the Food Zone for some Caribbean food, then The Cookie Lady Cookie Shop, assuring him that things will not always be so challenging. I brought him back home. We ate the cookies in silence in the car, watching homeless people argue over a bench at the curb before walking to the front door. Sharia never knew we left.

Chapter 5 – The Visitor

Howard Capelton

Lil DAP got into it with another kid at the after-school program.

Sept. 18

Victor Lovelett

How's he doing at school?

Sept. 18

Howard Capelton

Strange enough, better. One of the assistants at the after-school program told me that his troubles come from the extra attention he brings on himself, and that others give him naturally, because of me being around. When kids come up to me when I pick him up, he does get real annoyed with them. He's asked if I can pick him up from school sometime, too. I don't know if it's a good idea now.

Sept. 18

Victor Lovelette

How's he doing?

Sept. 18

Howard Capelton

Dude was totally rattled. His mother was up in her bedroom with "company" while Lil DAP was curled up in a ball in bed about it all. The blow up at the after-school program was another simple miscommunication where, if the mother wasn't so hard up to be in her room with this dude, she would have recognized it and straightened it out when she picked him up. Instead, she came up there, believed the first piece of an explanation from that sorry staff and smacked and slung the boy into the car.

Sept. 18

Victor Lovelett

Any words with her "friend?"

Sept. 18

Howard Capelton

Did what you said, remained calm, stressed that I am there for the kid, not the mother. He's your typical pants sagging bum. He came out of the room like he was going to do something, but calmed down. He mumbled something and pulled her on to go with him back into her room. I figured that Lil DAP's probably spending the night in his room alone, heating up some TV dinner to eat by himself, so I took him to get some food. We left the front door unlocked and didn't say we were leaving. She didn't call me or anything. When I brought him back, she didn't even come out to notice he had been gone.
Sept. 18

Victor Lovelett

What did you say to Lil DAP?
Sept. 18

Howard Capelton

It was more like what he said to me. He said he was tired of the hard time he was getting from trying all the things I was suggesting. He said he wanted to see me doing something hard. I messed around and told him about Karen.

Sept. 18

Victor Lovelette

Howard, what did you tell him about your sister?

Sept. 18

Howard Capelton

Don't worry, I said I lost my sister from complications from SIDS when I was young.

Sept. 18

Victor Lovelett

He wants to see you go through hard stuff and you went straight for the gusto.

Sept. 18

Howard Capelton

I'm having trouble sleeping again, but I still can't tell him everything of course. He just looked at me after I said it for a second like, "so, niggas die around me all the time." I guess he's right. I hate that whatever I could possibly say is easily trumped by some kid's life. What I'm dealing with is beyond serious. He caught himself and then said he wished he could have SIDS so he could go to sleep and wake up somewhere else.

Sept. 18

Victor Lovelett

Jesus. You alright?

Sept. 18

Howard Capelton

Yeah, he really needs his dad right now. I'm all he has. Tiff's starting to complain about my being away so much of the day on top of that. I would say that I'm not sleeping because of the infant thing, but its stress over Lil DAP, stress over Tiff, it's everything. I should have never responded to that email from 5000. Did you recommend me to them?
Sept. 18

Victor Lovelette

No, Howard. Your insurance company wants to look good in the black community. You're a young black professional on their team. They found out about 5000 Role Models and set it up for you to get an invite to join and now you're making an impact. I commend you. You're doing the work, my brother. There are men of the community who're football coaches, high school teachers, preachers. Everybody needs them everywhere, including their own families. Doing for the people is serious business. Be careful, Howard. I can't stress that enough.
Sept. 18

September 21, 2009

Journal:

Roman met me at the door before I could knock. It shocked me out of my sleep-deprived haze. He demanded to know my visitation schedule. David sat in living room with Effrom playing video games and stated that I was there to see him. Roman commanded David to "shut up". I reminded Roman that my business in the home was discussed the last time I came by. Roman advised me to watch my "tone." Roman closed the door on me. Sharia opened the door, and came outside, still in her work clothes, she apologized profusely for Roman's behavior. I assured her that this situation will not work and reminded her that unnecessary tension involving acquaintances in the home is enough for me to terminate sessions. I informed her that a termination would force her to spend more time with David. I spoke of his talk of dying to be in a better situation while she was in her room with Roman. Sharia quieted me and stated that David and Effrom were in earshot. Sharia assured me she had talked to David about his comment.

Sharia brought me inside. Roman was cursing in the kitchen. Effrom excused himself and told David he would see him later. Sharia stated that it was time to get something cooking for dinner and went into the kitchen.

I sat with David at the dinner table as Sharia began cooking and Roman, appearing to be in even more of a foul mood, went out on the front steps with a cell phone, slamming the door behind him. David appeared tense. I asked how everything was going with school and the after-school program. He said it was alright, stating that he "gets real close" to adults before he says all that "army slave mess" (ma'am, sir) to them. David spoke up and said he would never say that to Roman. Sharia appeared to have heard David, but said nothing. I said I understood. Sharia went out of kitchen after Roman. David admitted that the "after-school people" were now listening to his "words" more, but he felt that they were only doing it because I would call up there and start asking questions instead of Sharia who would just… He lowered his voice and motioned a slap alongside his head.

Sharia returned to kitchen. I asked Sharia for a glass of water, adding please at the end. Sharia insisted on me having Kool-Aid. Roman came through front door and stated that if water was what I wanted then that's all I should get. Sharia asked Roman how did he even hear what was said from outside. Sharia told Roman to go on in her room. Roman gathered some things and left with another slam of the door. Sharia brought me a glass of Kool-Aid with ice and slipped out of the kitchen (possibly to catch up with Roman). David said I did not have to say please to his Sharia because she "don't act right." David said she just argues with Roman then goes in the room with him a lot.

I advised David to always show respect to adults, even if they're "trippin'." David said he noticed Sharia says "army slave" words to important people. I asked if he thought I was important. He smiled and declared I was supposed to be important only to him and no one else. I assured him that his shoes were important too. He pulled the heels of his shoes from under the back of his feet. I asked him to hand me a napkin that was within his reach. I added please and a thank you, sir, to show him that he was important, too. David told me not to call him sir yet because he "was still just a boy" and that he "has to grow and do stuff that makes people want to say that to him."

I asked how David and Effrom were getting along. He said he discovered Effrom doesn't like Roman either and cannot read very well. David said Effrom likes to talk in class when David is asked to read out loud by the teacher. He said Effrom is a little nicer and keeps asking him how he knows so many words. I said that was interesting because a lot of kids who are so smart usually get teased that they are "acting white" when they do well in school, especially boys. David said Effrom was smart enough to see that reading well is good "so you know where the bus is going." He asked why kids make fun of smart kids. I said most kids are jealous that smart kids know and discuss things they can't figure out. I also shared that many kids think that smart kids are trying too hard to make certain adults, whites especially, like them by simply doing what they are supposed to do in class in the first place. I assured David that he would start hearing kids get teased like this soon enough. I stressed that this is why people tend to judge people based on the friends they choose. I stated that people are usually friends with each other because they think and act a lot alike.

I presented David with paper and color pencils. David said when Effrom saw my drawing of a Power Ranger, he stopped saying I was "gay." I instructed David to draw his very own super-hero. He laughed nervously and stated he could "draw good, but not enough for a hero." I assured him that he could. After several attempts, he came up with an amazing picture of Metal Man, a man that resembles a wrestler and an armored knight. Metal Man appears to wear Sunblocker-looking shades like "old people with bad eyes but these play ITunes and shoot lasers." Metal Man has long metal claws on each hand because he and X-men hero Wolverine "have the same daddy." He stated that Metal Man wears so much metal so he can't be shot or stopped and that no one can ever hurt him again. I asked how Metal Man was hurt the first time. He said Metal Man will never tell. I asked why not. David asked if I told him everything that hurt me before. Checkmate.

Sharia began frying fish. I asked what would be Metal Man's weakness. David thought long and hard. He eventually stated that he saw an old bike near his bus stop and that the chain on it was brown and crusty. He said he put his foot on the chain and it popped easily. I informed him that the chain was rusty, which was caused by rain or water. He stated that water would be Metal Man's weakness; if he cried or sweated because something was hard to do, his armor and weapons would rust and he'd be helpless. He eyed Sharia cooking and then looked over to me warily.

David asked what I had done as a kid that would make my father not like me much anymore. I remembered having said something along those lines during the previous session. I shifted in the rickety chair and said I had done stupid things as a kid and would talk about it at some other time. I asked where David's cousin Naomi and her infant were. David said she was up the street at somebody's house. He asked how a child would know if they have SIDS. I assured David he did not have it. I hugged David. I had to. I was passed the satisfaction of him needing me, of not always seeing me as the kid in the relationship. Now, it was different, as if he'd respect me now no matter what he would ever learn about me. The way I dream of it being with you, dad and mom. It must have been for him, too because he did not push my embrace away, yet did not hug back. I thanked him for such an awesome super-hero and asked if I could keep it. David gave it to me, said I was "like Metal Man a little bit," and continued to watch Sharia. I gave him dap and ended session.

Howard Capelton

It's not working with this dude that's over there. She's practically chosen this guy over her son.

Sept. 21

Victor Lovelett

Are we being fair in all this?

Sept. 21

Howard Capelton

I don't know. Maybe she's trying to keep the peace. I don't know. I was in the kitchen with Lil DAP and the boy says he would never say please and sir to this guy because he's such an ass. This dude came in the kitchen earlier complaining that he overheard her offer me Kool-Aid. I wonder if he overheard what Lil DAP said. Either way, I told the kid I completely understood and his mother heard me say it.

Sept. 21

Victor Lovelett

You're just asking to get something started.

Sept. 21

Howard Capelton

I hate violence, but… I don't mind me feeling like crap about myself. I do mind this kid I've been trying to build up, this innocent, talented kid gets messed up in this. He can really draw. He has talent.

Sept. 21

Victor Lovelett

What if that dude beats your head in? Or worse? What if he's the punk type that pulls a gun instead of knucklin' up?

Sept. 21

Howard Capelton

I don't really care. I can take whatever.

Sept. 21

Victor Lovelett

What are you saying, Howard? What are you really saying?

Sept. 21

Howard Capelton

The thing with all this is people with a nice job and all want to help as long as it's a clean situation. Something that looks good for a photo op. They want to wear latex gloves as they lend a hand out to people, and then walk off, trash the gloves and call it a day. I just feel like being all in for once.

Sept. 21

Victor Lovelett

Admirable perspective, but I think there's more to what you're saying, or rather, why you're saying it.

Sept. 21

Howard Capelton

I don't know if it is possible to be a better man for the wrong reason.

Sept. 21

Victor Lovelett

I know where you're going with this. I don't like it.

Sept. 21

Howard Capelton

Lil DAP asked me if there was anything I could have done to make my father not want to talk to me. Clearly I do. I know what I did, but my dad doesn't. So I've been enjoying a relationship, a life, I really don't deserve.

Sept. 21

Victor Lovelett

Howard come on, man. Everybody has personal demons. Everybody has regrets. Do you think I would be bothered about you if you were not worth the trouble? And I know everything!

Sept. 21

Howard Capelton

This kid is innocent and his mother's stuck on stupid and his ass of a dad won't even pick up the phone. To top it off all this other crap is happening to him. I would have snapped a long time ago if I was him. How can an adult who is weaker and more spoiled than a child be some kind of role model or sense of foundation to that same kid?

Sept. 21

Victor Lovelett

You're a lot stronger than you think. Having a conscience does not mean you're weak. It just means you have a strong sense of justice which, when not put into context, can cause more harm than good. The only way you can keep him from losing it is to make sure you don't do so yourself. I'm about to call you. Answer your phone.

Sept. 21

September 22, 2009

Journal:

I drove to David's while practicing deep breaths. He was in sweatpants and an old T-shirt two sizes too large. He asked if I was taking him to karate. I said yes. He gave me dap and karate kicked me in the leg, pulling his foot back slowly to show his shoes were on properly. I heard the cry of David's infant second cousin in Sharia's room. I leaned against the door frame. I asked if Roman was present. David said no and suggested I learn karate too, so we could "beat that n**** up in a tag team." I asked if he meant "apple." David said, "he ain't no apple, he a n****." He said Roman "calls me one, so he one back." I asked if everything was okay other than that. He said Sharia and Roman "drink beers and argue" (David calls all alcoholic drinks beer) and that he can't ask Sharia too much or else she will yell. He then said he asks her if he can call me to see what I'm doing and Sharia calms down a little. He sighed and said he just wishes she would not drink beer so much and that Roman would go somewhere and die.

The infant continued to cry. David asked if I was ready to "hold the baby til' you sweat?" I admitted to feeling uncomfortable about crying infants. He asked me if I thought that the infant had SIDS since she was crying. I said no and told him everything that deals with small children is not SIDS so he does not need to focus on that all the time. I said there was so much else involved with having a child. He assured me that good people figure it out. I asked if he was sure. David said yes, and asked suddenly, or stated perhaps, that I "must wanna get a baby for real." Before I could respond, David said if my wife's "face get big and shiny" and she "throw up a lot," then I would get one soon. This kid is amazing.

I said Tiffany and I were still just talking about it. I assured David that he would make an awesome father when he grows up. He was quiet as I drove him to karate class. I asked what was wrong. He said that he hopes my wife is not pregnant because then I would stay in my house and sweat over my baby and forget about him. I gripped the steering wheel and said I would not do that. He sighed heavily, as if not completely convinced. I pointed to Tupac, now in a mesh bag the size of a child's footie sock dangling from my rearview mirror. David smiled.

I told him that when I get different ideas on things to do with him or show him, I also try those things on myself to build character. David asked what character was. I stated that character makes people the type of people they are when no one is watching. I gave an example that there are people who will not steal not because it's wrong, not because too many people are watching them. I stated that people have character when they do the right thing – even if nobody else is around to see it. He said I "had enough character already" since I come to see him. I almost said I wish. Instead, I said I always strive to be a better person. Real BS. He said maybe I was "just gettin' enough character for two kids" (meaning David and my possible future child).

I watched David closely in karate class. He seemed more focused on my approval than he was last time. He looked back to me after every other punch and kick for affirmation. He was a bit hesitant about yelling "kiai" with every strike, even raising his hand to inform instructor that "people don't fight like that for real." I encouraged him to take to the instructor's guidance a little better. He did so, accepting the push-ups he was given when not paying attention with a sigh instead of stomping his feet and refusing to as he did before. The instructor complimented him after class on his improved behavior.

As we headed past the old Ace Theatre on Grand Ave, I emphasized focusing all of his anger in the "kiai" yell of karate during strike. David responded with a "yessir" and practiced his "kiai" yell as he punched at Tupac the ping pong ball, stopping within inches of connecting. I considered David's reaction to news of me possibly having a child and suggested he punch and "kiai" at passing cars. I arrived at the apartment. He looked light-headed and asked if people with character forget their friends. I assured him they do not, gave David a bear hug, and ran my hand over his tight, nappy hair. I hugged that damned boy like he had my nine year-old self hidden inside of himself. I ended the session. Tiffany, this is what you're pushing me to.

September 24, 2009

Journal:

I drove to Fairchild After-School Program in the rain, passing by some of the old shotgun houses on Charles Ave, Miami's oldest residential street. I waved to Nassau Daddy, the sculpture of the silly bird dressed as a Royal Bahamas police officer off Douglas and Grand Ave. Got my first and only public ass-whooping from ma there. Too many memories. The cussing and fussing on porches during barbecues. The colorful Junkanoo costumes, feathers, whistles, horns and drums for Goombay. So much conch salad and shining, 'round-the-nipple-dark-colored people, with egg shell-colored teeth showcased from burgundy wine-colored gums. Back when you could see the untouched African in shapes of heads and noses, whether they claimed it or not. Back when last names meant something, when someone could look in your face and run down if your people were from the Gibson or Stirrup family line. Now, too much peeling paint and warped-shingled roofs claim homes. Too much talk of who got shot near Gil's Spot or Pine Inn dilute the flavor. And, of course, there's always that other thing. It all kills me and welcomes me all at once.

I reprimanded David about walking on the backs of his shoes when I got there. He said school was "a little different" because a substitute teacher was teaching today. He said his classmates were trying to lie to the substitute to trick her into letting them eat snacks whenever they wanted. He said that a boy went to the teacher's desk and told her the truth. He said another male peer called him a "punk snitch" for doing so. I asked what did the boy at the desk say about it. David just sighed and spoke of noticing that the only people other than the boy at the desk that tried to inform substitute teacher on how their regular teacher "usually do stuff" were girls. David said only girls can be "snitches that way" so he kept quiet so he wouldn't have to "punch somebody in they face" and get in trouble later. He admitted that he knew I expected him to "say stuff" to help the substitute, but that he had "enough to think about already sometimes."

I took him home. Naomi opened door with that infant in her arms. I petted it before David said anything. He shook his pinball-shaped head and smiled at me, "she ain't no snake, man." I pecked the infant on the forehead with a kiss and presented him with a game from a bag I was holding called Operation. His cousin remarked that she remembered her grandmother having that game. I assured David the game had been around that long because it's that good.

I set the game up on the kitchen table. Naomi sat in to play along, holding the infant in her lap. I explained to David that the object was to reach into the small, metal-rimmed cavities of game board with a pair of tweezers to take out miniature replicas of bones. Naomi interrupted, saying that if the tweezers touched the metal rim of cavity, then a buzzer would go off and David would lose his turn. I told him that whoever has the most retrieved bones in the end wins.

David enjoyed the game, although he had trouble settling his hands he even attempted to hold his wrist with his free hand for extra help. After several games, he became a bit withdrawn from consistently losing. Naomi told him it was very childish to pout, that no one wins all the time. Her phone started ringing and she went off with the child to answer. The infant gurgled as if choking on spit the whole time. We practiced the breathing and counting technique several times. I then played David again. David noticed his hands were now more steady.

David won a game and regained some confidence. I emphasized that he should use breathing techniques whenever he needs to – even if that means asking the teacher to get a drink of water to do it in the hallway or to put his head down on his desk and do it. I also had David revisit his behavioral contract drawn up on September 9th session. He restated that he was good in school so why bring it up. I agreed and just stated that they were looking over it to see how well he had progressed since then. He laughed nervously and stated people don't ever "look back on things on paper" about him unless it was to show he was "messing up." I went over contract, restated that he had enjoyed karate and other outings as promised in the contract since he maintained good behavior. I shook his hand. I said I looked forward to even better behavior reports. David shook my hand weakly and stated, "You don't mean like, being good like a girl good. I can just be boy good, right?"

I shared with David that he noticed girls who get a little loud are called "tomboys" or are told not to act like that whereas boys are expected to be a little more destructive. He said he noticed teachers tend to get after girls more to "do good in school for real and just tell boys stop gettin' in trouble so much." I told David to never sink to such low expectations, that being stupid in school is not what being a boy is about.

I stated that as he got older, he would see twice as many girls going to college than boys, and that too many boys will then wind up in jail or worse because they don't have the education they need to make money and be husbands to the girls. "And fathers?" asked David. I stated, yes and fathers, because men like to think they're taking care of their family. I went on to say that when men can't get good jobs because of not having a good education, they start to wind up in court needing behavior contracts for themselves. He said he wanted to write the contract for them when he grew up. I gave David dap. I thanked him for his behavior, attentiveness and character – and ended our session. David, the overmatched biblical slayer of Goliath. At least Sharia named you right. I hope I'm the rock in your tattered sling.

Howard Capelton

Lil DAP has gotten hip to asking to call me when his mother and boyfriend treat him badly.

Sept. 24

Victor Lovelett

He's still a kid. Kids can push buttons and abuse things.

Sept. 24

Howard Capelton

Granted, the kid can be annoying, all kids can be annoying. All humans can be annoying, but he deserves better.

Sept. 24

Victor Lovelett

Has your agency contacted the mother to see about counseling she may need for herself?

Sept. 24

Howard Capelton

Haven't heard anything. It's amazing the pieces of the human experience this kid is putting together. He's seen and heard about enough females being pregnant to know the signs of one showing, yet has missed out so much on male guidance that even a screw up like me can become a hero to him.

Sept. 24

Victor Lovelett

That sounds like some screwed up modesty on your part.

Sept. 24

Howard Capelton

He's starting to put the pieces together on what Tiff and I having a baby could mean as far as my having less time for him. Things have never been so touch and go in his home life now that this bum is in his house, and yet, Tiff getting pregnant would basically leave him fending for himself.

 Sept. 25

Victor Lovelett

Can't you break things to him gradually?

Sept. 25

Howard Capelton

I can't bring myself to lie to him. Kids get too much of that, this one at least. I find it difficult to discipline him knowing the inevitable.

Sept. 25

Victor Lovelett

You can still visit the kid. It'll just be as a true friend. No job stipulations.

Sept. 25

Howard Capelton

You're right. It's not inevitable, I have a choice even though it would be different. And I know one thing, I'll never play ping pong again. He was wonderful in karate today. He was respectful and everything. We drove home and I got a call from his mother to hold back at some gas station because folks were shooting by the apartment. We got the call to come back. I'm driving through the complex, through red and blue flashing lights. He wouldn't even look out the window; me leaving him is more frightening than bullet casings and chalk outlines of bodies. He hugged me, too. How am I supposed to walk away from that?

Sept. 25

Victor Lovelett

Don't. Somehow, just don't.

Sept. 25

Howard Capelton

I played the old Operation game with him. He loved it.

Sept. 25

Victor Lovelett

They still make those?

Sept. 25

Howard Capelton

Lol. Yeah. I was amazed at how well he settled himself down to play. We then looked and talked about the behavioral contract I first drew up with him. He realized how he had improved over our months together.

Sept. 25

Victor Lovelett

You did that, Howard. That is you at your finest.

Sept. 25

Howard Capelton

It dawned on me, and him, that the sooner he improved and worked out all his issues, regardless of when Tiff gets pregnant, the sooner my file with him would close anyway.

Sept. 25

Victor Lovelett

So she's still getting more anxious about the time you spend with him? She was all for it when you started.
Sept. 25

Howard Capelton

I promised I'd stop to focus on our kid if she had one. I had to come up with something to stop the nagging. If he stays where he is behaviorally or does worse, he'll have me to lean on until the baby arrives. If he works through his issues, his time with me can be terminated even sooner than that. Where's the reward in that?
Sept. 25

Victor Lovelette

You truly have me stumped on that one.
Sept. 25

Sept. 26

Tiff:

What is your damn problem?! And don't say you're sitting at your sister's grave because I drove by Charlotte Jane Cemetery already. This isn't the way to react when your wife tells you she's pregnant. This is ridiculous, Howard. You keep yelling and pacing around everywhere and it's starting to scare me. We've been talking about starting a family for the longest, so what's the problem? You said you can't stand women like that boy's mother who're all drama, that you like that I'm not drama. Like I was saying when you stormed out, I chose you because you have it all together already. You're educated, good-looking, kind... and yes, safe (the safe that I want). How is being called safe an insult? If you were messed up I wouldn't have picked you. You've done well for yourself so stop pissing me off! Stop pissing us off.

10:39 p.m.

Tiff:

I'm sorry, ok? Where are you?

2:36 a.m.

I'm at a hotel. I need space. I'll be back in the morning.

2:40 a.m.

Tiff:

What hotel?

2:41 a.m.

Just chill.

2:45 a.m.

Tiff:

Everything in this relationship is you pushing me into it. I didn't like the house, but you wanted it. I hate that couch but you had to have it. You're too comfortable with assuming I'll go with anything you say because you think that's what a husband is. It's not.

7:03 a.m.

Tiff:

Be a man and answer the phone!

7:45 a.m.

Tiff:

I hate you.

7:52 a.m.

You don't even know me. I'm going into work for a while.

8:03 a.m.

Tiff:

Am I wrong to assume you're coming home for lunch?

3:31 p.m.

Tiff:

Howard?

3:45 p.m.

I'll be there for dinner.

4:20 p.m.

September 28, 2009

Journal:

It was pouring down hard again. I drove to after-school program thinking to get David a rain jacket. He had taken a jacket from his school's lost and found the prior week. He became hostile with a peer who eventually recognized jacket as his own. He had come close to getting into a fight with several friends of the peer's while sitting in the cafeteria because of being questioned and teased about the rain jacket. He apparently took off the jacket and threw it in the boy's face, telling him to keep it. The wind started picking up, so Sharia, in an unexpected maternal mood, feared he would get sick.

David ran through the hard rain into the car. I reprimanded him about the backs of his soggy shoes being stepped on. Why do I even bother (with anything for that matter)?! I asked him what's the point of joking about all the people in Florida wearing flip flops if he treats regular shoes the same way. He asked me not to turn on the AC so much, then asked where we were going. I said we were going shopping to find him another jacket. He asked if it would be a nice jacket, "like a Timberland or something" because he had been laughed at a lot at school for using the lost and found jacket. I said it would be a decent jacket and that he should be thankful that he would have one of his own. He complained that I could buy a Timberland because I "got money like that." I advised him that being picky about something he was not getting anywhere else will have him with no jacket at all.

When I pulled into the parking lot of the local Kmart, David threw his head back into his seat. I reprimanded him about his attitude and asked if he wanted to just go back to the after-school program and not have session for the day. He folded his arms and his nose turned red. I said that he needed to work on his disrespect if he expected to get anywhere in life. I told him that we would sit in car he straightened himself out. After seven minutes, he complained that he had been sitting in the cafeteria sharing tater tots with his

171

"girlfriend" and some boy from another class told him to give up the jacket and that he had stolen it.

David said he called the boy a liar. The boy got teacher involved. The teacher had David take off jacket. David opened jacket and on the inside of collar and saw that the boy's name was written with a marker. He told David to "quit stealin' people stuff." David grew angry and threw the jacket in his face. David admitted that he had boasted that his "play uncle" would "buy a jacket mo' better anyway." He said that a crowd of laughing kids pinky bet him that he would get a "sorry" jacket. He said the kids stopped bothering him, but that if he came to school with a sorry jacket he would have to fight someone and get in trouble in order to make them all leave him alone. I drove to Burlington Coat Factory store and purchased an LL. Bean jacket. He complained that nobody at school "care about no Burlington Coat Factory." I told him he was getting on my nerves.

I insisted on not buying a Timberland to prove a point, that this jacket was nice all on its own and David should not think certain brand names on clothes mean everything. He mumbled thank you and did karate punches and kicks with jacket on as I walked him out of store. He seemed lethargic in karate class, whining about how cold his feet were, then about needing to blow his nose after working himself up to more tears. I called out for David to straighten up. The karate instructor asked me not to speak out to students or else all the parents would follow suit. Sharia came in later on with Roman. She had on her work clothes and said that Roman had gotten himself a car, but it needed transmission work. She admired the jacket I had brought him and hugged me. Roman scowled. I had to conclude the session, leaving my seat and giving extra space to Sharia and Roman. I told Sharia to tell David that he has a nice front kick and that the wife and I were indeed having a baby.

Chapter 6 – Divided Loyalties

 Howard Capelton

You were right. My boss admitted to contacting 5000 Role Models to recommend me. Oh yeah, Tiff's pregnant.

Sept. 29

 Victor Lovelett

Don't act like you didn't play a part in it. Lol Congratulations!

Sept. 29

 Howard Capelton

That means nine months to get my head and this kid's situation together. He may be a little too cool for my tastes. The boy is standing around at bus stops getting drenched from having no raincoat at all and actually requested I buy a Timberland jacket. Being dry is being dry last time I checked.

Sept. 29

Victor Lovelett

Please tell me you didn't buy it.

Sept. 29

Howard Capelton

Lol I got him an LL.Bean jacket instead, one just as good in quality without the 'hood fabulous status attached to the label.

Sept. 29

Victor Lovelett

That seems strange from a boy who is so careless with his shoes.

Sept. 29

Howard Capelton

It is. He treats all his clothes like garbage but then insists on a Timberland jacket. Maybe he's about to upgrade how he keeps his gear. His mother seemed thankful. Her little friend is apparently getting himself some wheels.
Sept. 29

Victor Lovelett

He may not be so bad after all. Once again, congratulations, man! Did you tell them Tiff was pregnant?
Sept. 29

Howard Capelton

Yeah. I should have waited. I hear most people wait for a couple of months, so they know there's no turning back. We'll see how things play out.
Sept. 29

Victor Lovelett

Remain prayerful.

Sept.29

September 30, 2009

Journal:

I ran into Mr. Poitier Gibson, a white-haired member of one of the pioneer families out by Charles Avenue. He was looking alright in a Miami Heat T-shirt, dungarees and straw hat for an 82 year-old. He and several others of the Revitalization Committee were out in front of the remade home of pioneer Mariah Brown and her husband, the first home built by a Bahamian in West Grove. The house is surrounded by a chain link fence missing the top rail. The yard is overrun with knee-high weeds. There was no way to tell the house was significant except for the faded white Early Settler sign out front by the Cemetery Commission. Mr. Gibson told me I looked exhausted. I said thank you, but only out of habit. He sipped on a can of Parrot coconut water, asked how the family was and when was I planning to join the committee and serve the way Ma and Dad still did. I said I was just starting to come back around, that I was working on it. He asked me what I needed to work on. One of the ladies, I believe it was Ms. Robinson, came up to him and asked him to help her locate something. I never did like her. The look she gave him over her bifocals took the voice from my throat. She looked at him as if to say he should know better, that he should *remember* why I wasn't around often, the he should just *know better*. I waved and drove off. Coming around is getting too close. Too much.

I got to the after-school program dry-mouthed and agitated. I greeted Sharia, who was walking in as I was. I asked if David was taking care of his jacket. She did not recall the jacket at first. I reminded her, to which Sharia remembered, apologized and said yes. Sharia said not to worry; she announced that she hadn't drank any today and blew in my face to prove it.

I asked how Roman and David got along. Before Sharia could answer, David came up and hugged Sharia and me. He was overly active, play fighting with peers. Sharia and I spoke with Mr. Sanford for an update on David's behavior. Sanford said he was less of the "offended avenger" and more of a careless trash-talker since receiving his jacket. Sharia warned David to stop horsing around several times. Sanford excused himself. Sharia seemed nervous and asked I several times how was my day. I said fine and asked how her job was coming along. She said she was always tired and that it was nowhere near enough to get off of assistance, but that she was doing all she could. I asked again how David and Roman were getting along. She hesitated and said that I was the best thing to ever happen to David, that she is working hard to "get right" with finances, living conditions, parenting, etc. She admitted that she may be too comfortable with people that "need to get right but don't want to" but that she would choose me over anyone in regards to her child's development. I said I would hold her to that since whatever male she keeps around is automatically involved in child's development

Sharia asked me to come outside just as it began to rain. We stood by the front. Sharia admitted to dealing with some "rough-cut types" concerning men in her life. I informed her that her son admitted to being worried because "when things get good she always finds somebody that make it bad." She attempted to laugh it off, but went silent when she reached out and caught some of the falling rain in one of her hands. She splashed the rain on her face and nodded. I said my impact is severely lessened when she allows abusive men into her home around her child. She sniffled. I asked if she had found a church home of some sort. She said no, but that she would "see about it." She washed her face in the rain again and cleared her throat. She said when David comes home from time with me "sayin' sir and ma'am" and "lookin' people in the eye when he speak" she can see what she should have been like around him all along. She then said, "I don't want him to go down with me if I cain't catch up in time." She asked me not to just forget her child when mine was born and went inside.

As soon as I entered, David bumped into me from chasing around a female classmate. He sneered at me. I asked if he had a problem. He rolled his eyes. I had him straighten his shoes and do push-ups for "tripping." (I told you I was agitated already) I followed him and Sharia to karate class. David was focused in karate class, complaining only on occasion. The head instructor brought David's karate uniform (which had just come in the mail) over to me and Sharia. Sharia asked me to be the one to put it on David. I declined and said I wanted to see her do it. She nodded, stood up and stated that she would be right back. She went outside for almost half an hour and came back with the smell of hard liquor on her breath. I tried to avoid eye contact with her.

Sharia asked how my wife was doing. I said fine. David began to look back at her (I believe he sensed she had been drinking). She motioned him to pay attention and asked me if I was "on her side" or if sessions with him was "just a j-o-b." I said I was trying to be on her side. He lost focus on a punching and kicking drill and began to complain that he wanted a drink of water. The instructor stated that he always whines for water when doing something he does not care for. I lifted up his uniform and said to the instructor that David would not be needing the uniform since he cannot do the exercises. That boy saw the uniform, forgot about the water and got focused.

As we watched the transformation, Sharia said Roman doesn't care for me but that's "too damn bad." She said she understood if any serious conflict arises between me and Roman that I must terminate sessions with David. She informed me that she didn't engage in sexual activity with Roman "much" when David was home. She admitted to bringing the incident in Richmond on herself by messin' with a "dope boy" and regrets how it affected her son.

I asked if Roman was a drug dealer. Sharia said she "hadn't seen anything" but that he has a P.O. (parole officer) for something. She said Roman said it was for "wildin' out back in the day." I asked if Roman had a job. Sharia said he works for a landscaping

outfit, "one of the last one's that ain't run by all these Mexicans" and needed extra cash
to get his transmission fixed. I committed the name of the landscaping company to
memory. I planned to check on it so she would know more about who she's having
around her son.

David began to spar with a peer per the instructor's instructions. He was a bit over-
aggressive. I assured Sharia that the best way to improve her son's life is to not deal with
that type of guy anymore. She asked if I had ever tried to fit in with a certain kind of
people but just "kept getting pushed back." She claimed she always laughs or talks too
loud or about the wrong things, or doesn't know what to say or wears the wrong thing the
wrong way. Sharia stated she starts conversations with sheriffs, teachers "and what not"
that come by the gas station, but they "just tryin' to play." I asked if she considered that
they noticed she was drinking when they talked to her. I stated that I tend to ostracize
myself from others before they get the chance to reject me.

Sharia asked what could a "clean little thing" like me have done that was so bad. She
slumped forward and warned me not to give her "another mush-mouthed answer" to her
question. I said I'd tell her soon. She begged me to tell her that I didn't "molest no damn
kids before or something." I said no, perhaps a bit too loudly. She threw the karate
uniform on the floor and complained that it "ain't right," that I must think I was "too
good" to share my life with her and her child. I picked up the uniform, grabbed Sharia by
the arm (she had leaned in too close) and told her I would tell her soon. "Don't speak on
my struggle 'til you speak on yours" she said and slumped back into her chair.

Karate class concluded. I explained to David that real karate fighters that wear the
uniforms do not complain about exercises. He stated that cool people would tell him
about new babies and not run away to make his mother do it. I ordered him to watch his
mouth. He walked away from me. Sharia appeared in agreement with him. She helped
him put on karate outfit and had another parent took their picture. The photographer

insisted I get in on the picture as well. David said no. I said fine, and concluded the session.

Howard Capelton

Well, he's mad at me for not having a sit down with him to announce that Tiff's pregnant. I didn't think it was that big of a deal. He's not treating his clothes and shoes any better either. I was always told that black folks who come up rough take extra care of their clothes. Lol

Sept. 30

Victor Lovelett

That seems to kick in during adolescence. Kids are usually free from all that crap until then.

Sept. 30

Howard Capelton

His mother finally admitted that hooking up with people trying to better themselves is a challenge to her. I believed she almost cried talking about it. It took me by surprise.

Sept. 30

Victor Lovelette

You think she was running game on you?

Sept. 30

Howard Capelton

Look at you! Sounding like a young dude! I sort of think it's truthful, but there's upwardly mobile females that get off on guys with an edge too so what you hear isn't necessarily the full reality.

Sept. 30

Victor Lovelett

A very mature assessment.

Sept. 30

Howard Capelton

In fact, I think she knows there's more to it than that. She went with us to his karate class and went outside for a drink while he was in there punching and kicking. He could tell she had been drinking and tried to ignore it. She actually said that she didn't want Lil DAP's life to be ruined just because she can't get hers in order.

Sept. 30

Victor Lovelett

As if the two could be separated at this point.

Sept. 30

Howard Capelton

Exactly! People think you can have a kid and continue hanging out in clubs and being stupid. Now that I think about it, she was probably pouring on the drama to see that I'll still be around after my kid is born so that she can continue being a part-time mother!

Sept. 30

Victor Lovelette

Going out on the town for a break with someone once in a while's one thing. Staying on a break in order to avoid parenting's an entirely different situation.

Sept. 30

Howard Capelton

She disgusts me sometimes. I suggested a church home or something, but she didn't seem too receptive. That bitch told me to not talk to her anymore about her struggles until I was able to speak openly about mine.

Sept. 30

Victor Lovelett

Whoah!

Sept. 30

Howard Capelton

I know! She's lucky someone decent's trying to help her and then tries to get picky with me! She said it after she had been drinking.

Sept. 30

Victor Lovelett

No, whoah to you. She clearly hit a nerve if she's a bitch all of the sudden. It's not a matter of being picky, it's a matter of trust. She's given you the very worst about herself, entrusted you to build her up from it as opposed to beating her down with it as others have done. She's looking to be trusted by you in the same way and know that you really can understand by sharing your struggle.

Sept.30

Howard Capelton

I cannot tell her. You know I can't.

Sept.30

Victor Lovelette

Tell her something. She probably knows you have no intentions of sharing it with her regardless of what you say and is resenting the imbalance in the relationship.

Sept. 30

Howard Capelton

You're making this sound so intricate.

Sept. 30

Victor Lovelett

What? Getting in-depth with motivations, concerns and the dynamics of relationships is something only for the educated middle class who can articulate it? Did you choose to help these people because you figure beggars can't be choosers? That they're in such a bad spot that they should accept whenever you demand things from them that you refuse to give?
Sept. 30

Howard Capelton

I just think they're missing what's important. If they were starving and I was offering them bread, what's the point of asking if I've eaten today?
Sept. 30

Victor Lovelett

The point is you're robbing them of the opportunity to care for you in return. Don't be patronizing. Gratitude alone can become demeaning to the person that was in need.

Eventually, pride and a sense of fair play arises, making the recipient desire to do something for you in return. In fact, some refuse whatever you offer them unless they know there is some sort of way to repay. It's their way of saying, yes I was down and low and you helped me up, but with this offering back to you I want you to know that I was and always will be just as much a man or woman as you. There are sorry people who just look to get over (meaning to get something without giving back in some way), the kind you always hear about that make projects and ghettoes the corrosive, depressing places they are, and then, you have proud people who're just in a sorry situation. Face it, Howard, from what you're saying it sounds like it's more of you dealing with proud people trying to struggle out of a sorry situation than you care to admit. When she slips and goes for a drink or the boy explodes at school, does that make you feel relieved that they appear to be pathetic and sorry? Is that the confirmation you need to feel superior enough to justify never opening up to them fully?

Sept. 30

Howard Capelton

I just have a lot on my mind. I'll talk to you later.

Sept. 30

Oct.1

> Tiff:
>
> *Have you given any more thought to us getting counseling?*
>
> *11:16 a.m.*

> *I'm going to the Lamaze classes with you. That doesn't mean anything?*
>
> *11:18 a.m.*

> Tiff:
>
> *Lamaze shows interest in the child, but we still have issues.*
>
> *12:10 p.m.*

> Tiff:
>
> *Hello?*
>
> *12:43 p.m.*

I don't get little breaks all the time at work like you. Still thinking about it.

1:40 p.m.

Tiff:

I heard what you said about worrying about my health and all that. Aside from low iron, I am fine and you know it. I know I told you I was going to chill with the birth control. Then you start up about not having a will yet. I think you're using anything you can pick up as an excuse to postpone having children. I would never try to put anything on you I feel you wouldn't want, but if we're going to do this, it needs to be done right. You can't "kind of sort of" raise a family.

1:44 p.m.

How you type all that mess so fast in text? Go to Facebook so I can type at my desk.

1:49 p.m.

Tiff:

Talking to text feature, genius. I guess talking on the phone is too much for you.

1:51 p.m.

Howard Capelton

I'm working on myself. I've been volunteering to get the feel of everything, but as soon as I get the feel of what I'm doing, here you come trying to shut it down. Nothing's fast enough for you. I have things I have to work out. I told you that. I told about that little girl they have over there that creeps me out. You don't respect anything I go through.
October 1

Tiffany Capelton

That's unfair. I can only respect and deal with what you tell me. If I knew you would be like this I wouldn't have married you.
October 1

Howard Capelton

You're a sales rep for Pfizer, Tiff. You met me in an urologist's office. I was getting a vasectomy so I didn't have to worry about kids while was out doing my thing. That's how you met me.
October 1

Tiffany Capelton

It's been six years. If you still wanted to do it, you would have anyway.
October 1

Howard Capelton

I said you were cool. I said I wasn't trying to get into anything serious, that moving in together was rushed, that I didn't want that ugly couch you bought, that we didn't have to get married so fast. You always figure if I get into something you want I'll just get used to it. You can't leave anything the way it is. Where's this going? Where's that going? Everything doesn't need to be flicked over, picked at and made into something else.
October 1

Tiffany Capelton

You won't face anything otherwise. You talk about that boy naming everything Tupac, you're more on a death kick than Tupac: Baby, I did this assessment on this family that died in a plane crash… Baby, I'm the worst, I killed a dummy I did CPR on. This fool almost hit me at the light up the street, I need a will. Tiff, my sister would fall out laughing in her grave at me having kids.

October 1

Howard Capelton

Chill with talking about Karen.

October 1

Tiffany Capelton

No, you use that to keep from addressing the issue. Why would your late infant sister have a problem with you raising a family? Did she tell you in baby talk kids are annoying? You don't make any sense. I think I bring life into your life and the commitment and responsibilities that come with it scare you to death. People who care for you will not wait for you to give them permission to help you deal with things.

October 1

Howard Capelton

I'm exactly who I've always been. You just hear what you want to hear. There's more to me than this corny suburban life you want for me.

October 1

Tiffany Capelton

You said I made you a better man.

October 1

Howard Capelton

I'm supposed to say that.

October 1

Tiffany Capelton

If you're going to deal with me, there's no way around not dealing with yourself. I gotta work. Get your mind right before you even dream of coming at me that weak again.

October 1

October 1, 2009

Journal:

I contacted Westco Landscaping's owner to discuss Roman. The owner (a friend of my family) stated that Roman worked steadily with company for several years but did not seem to be getting on the job lately because of reduced hours. The owner said his company is "going through it" in regards to the economy and simply cannot use all the workers full time that it has presently. He said eight or so workers have worked with company longer, so their seniority and work record give them top priority. I thanked the owner for his time.

I contacted Roman's parole officer (Roman served time for armed robbery) and informed him of the situation at Sharia's home. Parole officer said "talking trash to a kid is sketchy at best" but did admit that threatening me, the mother and/or child could make it so that losing a job would be the least of Roman's concerns. The parole officer admitted that Roman can be a "hot head" and has been "spotty on checking in lately." He gave me his phone number and said he would attempt to contact Roman before David's next session.

October 2, 2009

Journal:

I received word during lunch that David lost his damn jacket. I had calmed down pretty much by the time I drove over there to pick him up to see the movie *"Where the Wild Things Are."* Roman answered door. He remained in the path to block me from coming inside and called David to the door. My fingers are shaking as I type this just thinking about it again.

David walked out of door rolling his eyes and chewing a chocolate bar so huge that he could barely keep his mouth closed. When we got in the car I asked if everything was alright. He attempted to swallow all of the chocolate, wiping spittle from the side of his mouth. I apologized for not telling him personally about my wife's pregnancy. He said Roman was a "****" (penis). He followed up with emphasizing that Roman "really is for real." David asked if that is the way all men "get" when they're not boys anymore. I assured him that was not the case. He complained that he did not want to grow up, that all men do is yell and push people around. He worried that if he was "all nice" like me, men like Roman would bother him.

I asked if the principal (a male) at his school yelled and pushed people around. David hesitated, said no, but did say that the man would yell if you ran in the hall. I asked him about the karate instructor and the bus driver, all males. He relented, said "okay, okay," but bragged that if Roman got "stupid," he had a gang to back him up so I would not have to "do much about it." I reminded him about my warning about gangs. He said it wasn't a "gangedy gang" but merely several classmates that could fight that were now his friends. I explained that gangs are usually kids that hide within groups to do things they would never do on their own. David asked if I ever had someone I loved get hurt by some people. I realized he was speaking of Sharia's assault. He said people don't bother others when they know a bunch of people will kill them if they do. He said he wanted to feel like that, that he needed more "insurance" like that.

I apologized. I said I only wanted David to not make mistakes that would haunt him. He countered, "So, I'm gettin' haunted anyway." He complained that I kept saying all these "simple, easy things like them people at school" and that I never had to know what he knew. I stated that I knew I would not buy another rain jacket and then asked what he knew about that. He ignored it and said that saying nice words were "okay but they don't work always." He said "sir" and "please" don't keep Roman from being a **** (penis) and that that's what he was. He stomped his foot on the floor and told me that I "wasn't going to do anything about it neither. Won't shoot nobody, won't fight nobody." I tried to respond but David cut me off, grumbling that I ought to "just go and be with yo' dumb baby."

I pulled the car over, into some University of Miami parking lot and demanded David gather himself. He unbuckled his seat belt and claimed I had him "all buckled up in cars like some dumb baby." This fool taunted me, saying that pulling the car over "ain't nothin' either" and that "ain't no way" I know "5000 niggas and ain't one got a gun." I got out of the car and leaned against the hood. After about eight minutes of watching traffic, the sleep deprivation had me nodding back and forth. I got in the car. He said some car would hit them and I would be in trouble because I wasn't parked in a spot and he would not have a seat belt on and would "be dead." I loudly admitted to seeing someone I loved being hurt and not doing anything about it, so he needed to watch his damned mouth. I said something like, "I know you think you're in hell, that you're some cute kid the world's supposed to care about! It doesn't! Kids cuter than you die every day!" Terrible. Yes, I know.

I gunned the engine and said that being haunted by the event is why I "bothered" with his "silly ass", to help make up for it. David said my hands were shaking and I should breathe more. I insisted he buckle his seat belt, shut up and know that he was not getting any candy at theatre since he decided to choke himself "with that Costco-sized candy bar." We sat there with the engine running in silence for a few minutes, letting the cars pass. Don't ask me why. He buckled his seat belt. I remained quiet. He asked who the loved one I spoke of was. I said it wasn't important and drove on.

I reached movie theatre with David and watched "*Where the Wild Things Are,*" a movie about Max, a young boy who allowed his inability to articulate anger turn into a tantrum that made him wrestle his mother and bite her on the shoulder. As the mother reprimanded him, Max ran behind his house to a lake and sailed to an imaginary world full of monsters. The boy tried to get along with the monsters, but saw and caused only more hurt and alienation. Max realized how his temper affected his own family and returned home to make amends. As I drove David back home, I asked why Max refused to do what adults asked of him. David said the adults were not listening to him, that the mother was in the living room with the boyfriend (which she was) giggling too much when the boy wanted to ask her things. He said that was why Max ran away to his "gang of monsters" because his mom did not listen. I agreed and that Sharia had a lot to learn, too. He said adults don't listen to kids because they don't get in trouble if they don't.

I asked if Max really hated his mother (as he had said in movie). David said no, that Max was just mad. I asked him if he could imagine how Max's mother felt when Max ran away since she was responsible for him. He said maybe, but whatever she felt was what she deserved for always pushing Max away. He also said that Max running into a forest of crazy animals at night with no gun or sword was "dumb" and that if he ran into a forest, he would be "loaded like Metal Man." I asked what Max could have done instead of run away. He said Max should have went to his room for a while and waited for the guy to leave so he could talk some more with his mother. David said the movie was "straight" (meaning good).

I said that "gang" was not a good word to describe Max's friends or David's for that matter. I stated that when people hear the word gang, they think of criminals and become fearful, that police start to hassle the people in that group. "But," David countered, "stupid men still leave them and their house alone, right?" I explained that police are men, too. He said he and I would just explain to the police when they came. I repeated, as I often had that, perhaps, what he means instead of a gang is that he has friends who know how to defend themselves and that it is best to just call them friends. He added, "Friends that fight."

I asked if Roman was getting physical with him. He said he "just keep saying stuff." I asked what he had said. He said that Roman was sitting at the dinner table lighting a cigarette while he was eating dinner. Roman began flinging lit matches at him and calling him a "bastard." He said he did not know what the bastard word meant but it can't be good. David said he tried to pick the smoking matches from his plate and Roman told him not to touch them. He said Roman tells him he "won't ever be – a cuss word – and that he can see why my daddy don't ever call me 'cause…" He got choked up and looked out the window, letting the breeze cool his face. "I flicked a match off my corn and he grabbed me by my shirt and pulled it up in my face talkin' 'bout I drink up all the juice. He say I always be beggin' for everything. He didn't say everything, he said the cuss word, too. I hate that n****! I ain't playin'!"

I apologized to David for having that done to him. I said that Roman will get straightened out. I said I would have a talk with Roman. Why did I say that? I don't know. I couldn't stop myself. "And do what?" he asked, "Fight? He said he waitin' on you to come through. He said you ran behind him and you all in his business like a woman." My stomach went tight. The parole research. I thought about how useless I am, how little sleep I get. I told him not to worry about that. I repeated his term, "friends that fight." I explained that everything depends on the word one uses to describe it. I said apparently Roman is using the wrong words with him.

I took a deep breath as I got out of the car in front of his apartment. Something made me take note of the elderly man hobbling along the curb, the moon and stars overhead. As if it would be the last things my burning eyes would see. Jay-Z's "Money Ain't A Thang" played from one of the apartments on the ground floor. I recited some of the lyrics I thought I knew for confidence, messing them up completely. David asked again who was the loved one I watched suffer. He complained that I knew everything about him, but that all he knows is how my wife looks, that she's having a baby, that I "do insurance" and hang ping pong balls on my "car mirror." I went up the stairs with him, to his floor and assured him that that was a lot. I reminded him that he had just learned something new about me today (of watching loved one suffer). We got to the door. The glow of the living room light came through the cloudy front window. I listened for any low masculine voice on the other side. I heard nothing. David knocked. Sharia answered. David and I both sighed. I told him to go on when she opened the door. I gave him dap and concluded session. As I drove away, I noticed he had scrawled his name on the ping pong ball with a pencil and placed it in my seat.

October 2

Mr. Capelton:

I have scheduled a mandatory meeting with all the counselors on October 5th at 5:30 p.m. This concerns proposed requirements the state is preparing to issue to all in-home counseling facilities. Please make a note to attend with your updated DAP notes and IEP reports.

Eudonis Warner,

Lead Counselor

423 NW 27th Terrace

Ft. Lauderdale, FL 33313

Sunrise Family Services

305-***-****

Victor Lovelett

Still got a lot on your mind?

Oct.1

Howard Capelton

I messed up even more. I had a blow up with him in the car. He was still ragging on me about not telling him personally about Tiff's pregnancy. I was like, if I had a choice I wouldn't have the damn thing anyway. Then he asked me then why are you doing it? I really cussed this kid out. I can't even type it.

Oct. 2

Victor Lovelett

You don't want to have the child? You're cussin' the kid out, what's going on with you?

Oct. 2

Howard Capelton

Everything was fine and now with the pregnancy, it's like there's no turning back. She's saying I ain't a man because I don't react the way she wants and now this boy is doing the same. I'm sick of everyone.

Oct. 2

Victor Lovelett

I don't know what you want me to say. I stressed a lot when my first born came, he wasn't all planned like you young professionals do these days. Lol. I never thought about her terminating. By the time my youngest boy came, I was much more relaxed.

Oct. 2

Howard Capelton

I know it sounds messed up. I know. I just want some say in all this. Just did some background checking on the mother's friend. He's kept a job mostly. He has a parole situation. Seems to have been in a rut because his job's letting him go. Bad economy.

Oct. 3

Victor Lovelette

Were you supposed to be doing that?

Oct. 3

Howard Capelton

I don't know.

Oct. 3

Victor Lovelett

A lot of folks are acting out over this economy. You got men in the suburbs who come home and shoot their whole family because they've lost their jobs. What was he in for?

Oct. 3

Howard Capelton

Armed robbery. I don't think it was an economic thing, just a rep building thing. He admitted to as much.

Oct. 3

Victor Lovelett

It wasn't my intent to discourage you from helping Lil DAP and his family. I just want you to make sure it's coming from the right place in your heart.

Oct. 3

Howard Capelton

Yeah. I kind of felt like I got back one of my papers from you full of red ink. Lol

Oct. 3

Victor Lovelette

We're all forever learning.

Oct. 3

Howard Capelton

So what's one of your struggles?

Oct. 3

Victor Lovelett

(Benign Prostatic Hyperplasia or BPH) Prostate issues. I haven't been keeping up with my health checkups and now I have an enlarged prostate that has me going to the bathroom throughout the night. I get so tired sometimes that I become angry with myself. I know it's some part of aging, but it truly upsets me. I'm looking at retirement and uncertain about what my standard of living is going to be. I still don't wear seat belts like I should.

Oct. 3

Howard Capelton

You were talking about that when I was in your class! All these years and you're still going rogue with the seatbelts! Lol

Oct. 3

Victor Lovelett

A brother can be hard-headed. I truly believe that if my wife had not passed back in '02, I would have had this seat belt thing handled by now. Lol. How's Tiffany?

Oct. 3

Howard Capelton

We've been arguing. She looks like she's just sitting around waiting to wrap some noose around my neck and tie the other end to her ankle. It's nerve-wracking.

Oct. 3

Victor Lovelette

Be patient, Howard. I'd like to meet with you two one of these
days.

Oct. 3

Howard Capelton

Speaking of patient, Lil DAP lost that rain jacket I bought him! I was so pissed! He told
me he has a gang now and that they'll find him another jacket. He said since he has this
new gang now I won't have to beat up his mother's boyfriend by myself!

Oct. 3

Victor Lovelett

Lol. Imagine that, a grown man being beaten up by a bunch of fourth
graders.

Oct. 3

Howard Capelton

I told him gangs sound too criminal, like they're out only to hurt people. Naturally, he countered and said this one's different, this one's for protection.

Oct. 3

Victor Lovelett

That's how they all start out.

Oct. 3

Howard Capelton

Right. He says he had to do something since I can't do everything.

Oct. 4

Victor Lovelett

He really is preparing for you to leave him. Make sure you emphasize that you'd still like to be around.

Oct. 4

Howard Capelton

He proved his point for needing a gang by asking me if someone I loved had ever been hurt before. I thought of his mother, then Karen. I told him getting into gangs is a mistake, that he'll make mistakes that will haunt him. I could feel my voice sounding hollow, that I was just reciting crap that did not fully take his situation into account.

Oct. 4

Victor Lovelett

What did he say?

Oct. 4

Howard Capelton

He said he was getting haunted anyway. We watched a movie together and talked some more. I'm going to open up to them some more, gradually.

Oct. 4

Victor Lovelett

I know you will.

Oct. 4

Howard Capelton

Speaking of that, I appreciate you telling me about yourself but I feel like David. I believe there's more about your struggle than just being in Baltimore and not having a father. You're so insightful about all I'm going through that it scares me. My father isn't even as accurate. I might be wrong that there's more to your story, but I don't think so. I'm going to ask you this one time, man to man, what else is there?

Oct. 4

Victor Lovelett

I grew up with just me and my mother and my little brother. Didn't like sports so I searched for a male mentor of some sort wherever I could. Mr. Earl, the neighborhood barber, seemed to look out for me. I was amazed how his afro never seemed to be out of place. I wanted to look clean and sharp like him. He looked like a young Gordon Parks, Jr. He never seemed to need a shave, like God stuck a perfect mustache on an otherwise smooth mug and froze time. He gave me free haircuts from time to time when momma couldn't pay. I dreamed of being a barber one day and figured I could start hanging out at the barber shop, help him close up after hours. I got two years of molestation for it.
Oct. 4

Victor Lovelett

You want more?
Oct. 4

Howard Capelton

Yes. Please.

Oct. 4

Victor Lovelett

The more he would come to my house and tell my mother he would have money for me to wash his car, sweep his stoop, or clean around the shop, the more I protested going, which made her believe that I was just a fourteen year-old punk avoiding honest work. So she beat me and practically walked me to his stoop, or the barber shop, dragging me by my wrist, convinced she was doing right by me. So no one listened. Nobody. Imagine that, I do wrong in school from acting out over what's being done and get sent to him to get straightened out about it. He had a chair off in the hallway, away from the storefront window. He would turn up the radio and shave me and do things to me. Do you understand what I mean by shave? Shame kept me quiet.

Oct. 5

Howard Capelton

I'm sorry. Shame keeps me quiet, too. Even the victimizer's in
shame.

Oct. 5

Victor Lovelett

I graduated from high school, got a barber's license and took some community college
courses until I cut enough hair to piecemeal my way into Morgan State. When I was
finally admitted as a full-time student, I celebrated by giving a dope fiend all the money
I had gotten for my book voucher, $236.53, to cave Earl's head in one night as he locked
up his shop. I didn't have the heart to do it myself. So Earl was left paralyzed, but I
didn't let it go. I started taking it out on my mother for not protecting me. Didn't even
go to her funeral when she died of breast cancer. Naturally, most of the family, who
think college folk are uppity, blamed my attitude on being educated, so that destroyed
my ties with most of my family. Went on through college, pledging a fraternity and
being so overzealous with hazing I left pledgees with broken clavicle bones, ruptured
ear drums and scars from putting cigars out on their bare chests.

Oct. 5

Howard Capelton

I remember you railing against hazing one time in class, but then you seemed upset with yourself because you said you just realized right then that it will never end.
Oct. 5

Victor Lovelett

The worthlessness I fought with was what I saw in you when you were in my class. I could tell you needed to make sense of the victimization and victimizing through education, to understand the impulses, to make it all less about you and more of a phenomenon you stepped into, to make peace with it. Suicide: You've talked about, I tried it. From half-assed Russian Roulette to driving into incoming traffic on a rainy night with the lights off and Bobby Womack blasting the speakers. Swerved out of the car's way only because it looked like children may have been inside. It's taken longer than you could ever know for me to find my place as a man among men.
Oct. 5

Howard Capelton

Among men, what do you mean by that?

Oct. 5

Victor Lovelett

Men who mean well, the kind of men who sought to school me on everything from looking people in the eye to firm handshakes were cursed out by me. Class advisors, big brothers in the frat, preachers… I insisted that all of them were as sick as Earl. I still haven't mended all the fences I've destroyed. I am still a work in progress.

Oct. 5

Howard Capelton

You don't seem like a work in progress from where I am. Your progress is so smooth. I'd be lucky if I have it together half as much as you.

Oct. 5

Victor Lovelett

No, you've caught me at a more enlightened phase. Even now, it's both liberating and annoying to type all of this out. It's past midnight. I need my rest, Howard. This is why I know so much, so well. Don't be me, be better than me.

Oct. 5

October 5

Mr. Capelton:

I'd just like to say that the impact you have had on David thus far is a shining example of what SFS is all about. It grieves me that the state is trying to push out so many hard-working people like yourself with these extras classes and degree requirements. As I said in the meeting, the new requirements are not likely to go into effect until next August. We desperately need more black men. Boys like David are so used to tuning out black women trying to reach them. Are you sure you can't take a couple of online courses?

_____

Eudonis Warner,

Lead Counselor

423 NW 27th Terrace

Ft. Lauderdale, FL 33313

Sunrise Family Services

305-***-****

Chapter 7 - Beyond the High and Pretty

October 5, 2009

Journal:

I drove to David's home for a late session. Sharia greeted me. She said Roman was out with his friends and she had a headache. Before she could say anything else, I told her that she had a point about me opening up to her and David. I told her that I love the smell of bacon cooking and wished there was a bacon air freshener for cars because I would buy it. Sharia said she likes bacon too, but likes drinking milk after chocolate cake more. I admitted that I dislike the Miami Dolphins because they don't give their black players as big of a contract as they do other players. I admitted I had only been to the Bahamas twice by way of cruises, but that I was Bahamian and didn't want any back talk about it. Sharia laughed and said I was probably Bahamian-American, maybe. She said she liked tennis, but would probably never try it. I told her I was the champion at holding my breath as a kid and could probably hold mine longer than anyone in the apartment building.

Sharia told me to stay put as she ran to her room. She returned with a letter from David's father, Roderick. I took a picture of the letter with my phone and retyped it:

David,

You don't understand what I got going on here. It's a lot. I send money for you to your auntie but I hear they keep it. Whatever money I send is never enough. I ask how you doing but it's always an argument. I have a friend and she has two kids. One is a boy and one is a girl and they're always into something. It keeps me very busy and tired. I think you're getting used to South Florida the way I'm getting used to them. You'll think about Virginia less and less. You needed a fresh start somewhere different. When it's sunny, I think about Florida. I have your picture. You cool with me. This sounds messed up, but I have to find a way to be happy. It's not you. You'll be alright.

Dad

I sat down after reading it. Sharia, visibly upset, stated she will not tell David about the letter. I agreed. She dried her eyes and thanked me. She then stated that she does not have a job anymore. Sharia said the manager got her "schedule mixed up or something" and that he was "just rude anyway." Sharia assured me that she would find something, though me keeping an eye out for something for her would be "cool." I said I had gotten word that the state would be adding new requirements to in-home counseling, requirements that I may not have (possibly requiring a degree in psychology, which I definitely do not have). Sharia winced, massaged the bridge of her nose and mumbled that everybody is "so scared some ****as 'bout to make some money helping each other." She said it was alright because I "could just visit" David "without all them rules anyway."

David came from his room in good spirits, giving me dap. He asked me what he was going to learn about today. I thought for a moment and said he would learn about me. I said I liked Tyler Perry movies. He was unimpressed, "So. Everybody like Tyler Perry." He said he likes splashing people at pools by doing cannonball dives. He then asked if I ever "said whatever I wanted" like him and Sharia did. I said that I think before I speak, usually. David said when he grows up he was going to say what he wanted, like a lot of grown-ups do.

I asked if Max in the movie "*Where the Wild Things Are*" did and said whatever he wanted. David hesitated and then questioned why I asked about the movie we had seen during our previous session. I stated that it was because I had an assignment for him to work on. I said we would work on writing a letter to Max from "*Where the Wild Things Are*" in order to give him advice on how to treat his family and friends. He recalled how Max wrestled and bit his mother, ran away from home and was just "trippin'" in the movie. I told him to think of three things he would advise Max to do next time he gets upset. He said he'd tell everybody he's getting mad, then go breathe a lot, and if that doesn't work then, if people still don't help, go in his room to choke and punch his pillow until his fingers get tired (he could kick it too, if he knows karate). I asked David about the biting. He said that was just Max tryin' to act like the wolf costume he was wearing at the time. Sharia listened in from the kitchen as he said that he dreamt of having a costume like Metal Man for Halloween, going to bullies' houses, beating them up and taking their food and video games. I asked David if there were bullies in his life. He said all adults are bullies when they don't listen because they're so big. He said the bigger people are, the less they listen.

I questioned if smaller people (children) should listen a lot so that they don't make as many mistakes as adults do. David said he guessed so. He sat at the dinner table and began writing the letter. I helped again with his spelling. He then asked me to help him draw more pictures of Metal Man. I began to draw one. I asked what does Metal Man do to have fun and what was his "regular job. " He said Metal Man goes to Chuck E. Cheese and birthday parties sometimes but does not dance and act "all dumb" like Chuck E. Cheese. He said Metal Man just eats pizza and cake and thumps kids and adults upside their heads when they act up with his metal thumb. Sharia, David and I laughed, together, for the first time. I told him he needs to be a comedian. David said he might be funny, but Metal Man wouldn't say a lot of funny things. It was a good moment. I prayed they would always remember me this way.

I asked if Metal Man had a family. David thought long and hard and said not yet. He said Metal Man had lots of girlfriends and helps kids where he lives so much already but when Metal Man did have a child it would be a boy that had his first name. He studied the picture I had drawn of Metal Man and stated the super-hero would not leave his son for long periods of time. He said Metal Man would do what "he gotta do" then come home "every time." I asked if that was what David would do when he had a family. He said yes and added that he would tell his family things about himself so they would know him instead of just come in and make them "take baths, go to their room and clean up stuff."

Sharia sat at the table with us. I let David keep my Metal Man picture. I then talked about working as a telemarketer for the Fraternal Police Organization when I was in college. I told him that I went to Florida A&M University for college. He said since I work two jobs, I must be rich. I explained that I work so hard because I was determined to buy my parents a new house not far from where I live now, a dream I had since I was a child. I shared that they were always helping kids in the neighborhood because they wanted the large family they never had. He said his mother should get two jobs. He said Sharia doesn't work at the gas station anymore. I told him I had heard.

David said he would like a little brother and that I could bring my baby over, even if it's a girl. I said I hoped my child would be as smart as him. He said the child could be smart like him "but not all the way like him" because then I would forget him. David said he would run away if I did that. I said I would not forget him. For some reason we all were quiet for a moment, like we sensed this was a still a goodbye of some kind. I thanked him for all of his thoughtfulness, concluded the session and said I would see him soon. Is it possible to be a child and know too much?

October 7, 2009

Journal:

You must show this to the police after you read it.

I drove to the after-school program to meet David. He came running to me blinking fast and holding his back pack tightly. He said Sharia and Roman were fighting that morning over her car. He stated that Sharia needed it to find a job and Roman needed it, too since his was still "messed up." He said Sharia threw keys at Roman. He said Roman "said a lotta apple words" and threw a flower pot that hit Sharia in the back. He said he yelled at Roman, who dared him to do something. He asked if I had a gun. I informed him that I did not have one. He seemed stunned, then cleared his throat and smiled. He said he didn't think I did "for real." He had this dry, cough of a laugh and said I would still be his friend. He asked for my phone number. Tiffany, I gave the boy my number to the office instead of my cell. It felt like I put poison in his food.

I said I would talk to Sharia. David asked when I would know if SDS would "fire" me "from seeing" him. I recalled telling Sharia in the previous session about new requirements for in-home counseling being instituted, which would keep me from continuing with him. I said I did not know but planned on visiting him like a regular friend anyway. He patted me on the arm heavily as we sat at a red light off Douglas Road and, as if realizing I was made of flesh and bone, bear-hugged me. I asked how school had been. He shrugged his shoulders and held on tightly. He growled as if trying to clear his throat while shaking me. I hugged him back. The light went green. I was moving.

I had David fix the back of his shoes. I called Sharia's phone. She did not answer. He seemed unusually calm as we sat at another intersection. "You scared?" he asked. Before I could answer, he went on. "Yeah, you are. Wish you didn't know me anymore, right?"

David shook his head and unlocked his door as if looking to get out. I told him to stop it. I said he shouldn't have to go through such foolishness but hanging out on street corners will not help. He sucked his teeth, looked into the sun and squinted his eyes. "Don't worry," he said, "I'ma be big one day." He squeezed the strap on his backpack and commented further, "I'll be an adult, then I won't need you or nobody like this." I argued that everyone needs each other. He nodded, "maybe." I tried to object. He resigned with a polite smile, as though arguing was useless.

I knocked twice, then turned the knob to see that it was open. Roman stopped us as I opened the door. David called for Sharia. Roman told him to shut up, saying that Sharia was asleep. Roman let him slide by to get inside. I asked to see Sharia. Roman pushed me back outside. I asked if everything was okay. Roman tapped me on the bridge of my nose with a finger and commented that he was "gettin' 'bout sick of" me. I assured Roman that the feeling was mutual. Roman shoved me and asked me what I was going to do. Roman stated that he had heard that I had been "everywhere" asking people about his business. Roman dared me to step to him as a man if I had a problem with him instead of running around like a ***** (female dog) asking others about him. He shoved me and dared me to ask anyone else about him again. I called out for Sharia. Roman dared me to call out to her again.

David yelled that Sharia was "moving slow" in her room. Roman punched me in the chest. I laughed and reminded Roman that he just hit a man as opposed to a woman, so he had better come with more than that. He punched me in the nose. I began to tussle with him. I could hear David coming yelling to Sharia that we were fighting. David yelled for Roman to get off of me. We continued to wrestle at the front door. He was still on top of me and had me in a headlock. He muttered that he would kill me. I blacked out and came to when the police arrived. Roman was gone.

Victor Lovelett

Earth to Howard. Do you copy? Haven't heard about you and Lil DAP lately.

Oct. 8

Tiffany Capelton

Dr. Lovelett, this is Tiffany, Howard's wife. I know that he confides in you about a lot of things. I found you on his friend's list. Something terrible has happened. Please call me as soon as possible. ***-***-****

Thank you

Oct. 11

9-Year-Old Boy Kills Mother's Boyfriend

Roman Jackson, who was killed by girlfriend's son.
October 15, 2009

(AP) Police in the West Coconut Grove community are looking into circumstances involving a 9-year-old boy who is charged with killing his mother's boyfriend with a .22-caliber pistol, the police chief said Saturday.

The boy apparently traded a rain jacket with a classmate and member of the boy's "gang" for the handgun. The trade shows premeditation, yet the boy allegedly shot the victim in the midst of an altercation at the home, Police Chief Charles Danville said. The mother's boyfriend got into a physical altercation with the nine year-old's mother and in-home counselor.

"Nobody's jumping to conclusions," he said Saturday. "This is unique in that the counselor went so far as to confess to shooting the boyfriend in order to protect the boy. Although the boy has a history of anger management issues and other behavioral problems, we have to look into the charges of abuse the counselor brought up. This kid's

9 years-old and already had his fair share of trouble, but taking the fall for the crime's such a large step for the counselor to take. This has lots of layers."

A judge determined Friday that there was probable cause to show the boy fatally shot his mother's boyfriend, Roman Jackson 31, from Overtown. According to Florida law, charges can be filed against anyone 10 or older. The judge ordered a psychological evaluation. The boy or mother had no record of complaints of violence in the home with Florida Child Protective Services, said Miami-Dade County Attorney Cynthia Suarez.

"He and his mother suffered a violent attack in Richmond, Virginia by a rival gang of the mother's then ex-boyfriend before they moved to Florida," Suarez said. "In fact, they moved here for a fresh start to put it all behind them." Danville said that, due to the complexities of the case, police are investigating possible abuse.

Police had no records of domestic violence calls at the Troy home, but the counselor has provided records of counseling sessions where of the child spoke frequently about it. "We're looking at this from every angle," Danville said.

Danville said officers arrived at Sharia Troy's home, the boy's mother, within minutes of the shooting Wednesday. They found the victim walking away from having crashed Troy's car by the old segregation wall between Main Highway and LeJeune Road. He had been shot in the shoulder and leg and had a gun of his own in his pants. An elderly man had called and said he saw a man "laid out by the wall bleeding out the leg like a hog," Suarez said. The counselor and mother remained at the residence with minor injuries. "The child sat at the kitchen table with some comic book hero drawing, apparently trying to call his father," said Danville. Jackson had been living on and off at the Troy residence, prosecutors said. The ex-felon was an employee of Westco

Landscaping and was reported to have been distraught over the company's likelihood of going out of business due to the economy.

Danville said police got a confession from the counselor, but it proved inconsistent with the evidence. A confession from the boy was forthcoming, but the boy's attorney, Harold Goldman, said police overreached in questioning the boy without representation from a parent or attorney, nor did they advise him of his rights.

"They became highly aggressive in the interview," Goldman said. "Two armed officers leaning over you talking loud and fast is scary for anybody. Imagine what it's like for a 9-year-old kid." Prosecutors are unsure of where the case is headed, Suarez said. "We've got a million factors to consider, the juvenile's age, and yet, there is this act that he apparently committed."

With gang activity growing in South Florida, officials are considering if the outcome of this case will serve as a message to youth involved with gangs. "It baffles the mind to comprehend that a 9-year-old fully understands the act of murder and its implications," Goldman said. "It's a legal minefield if they prosecute him. Everybody will have to decide if we want to use the criminal justice system to deal with 9-year-olds who really just need more guidance in the household."

The mother had full custody of the child. The boy's paternal grandmother has come from Richmond, Virginia since the shooting, Suarez said. Goldman said the boy is mannerly, draws his own made up comic book hero and tries to meditate. "He's still scared though," he said. "He constantly asks to see his counselor and is trying to be tough, but he's scared."

October 16, 2009
Family, this Damn Ping-Pong Ball,

I have lived freely for long enough. There is no sacrifice that is clean. There's always the collateral. I made a horrible mess before and I tried to clean up a potential mess this time. I had good intentions. I know in my heart what I was trying to achieve. I told David what I did when I was his age, who I hurt. I told him in his ear just as the police were taking him away. We share a common ugliness, mine still worse than his.

He is a boy having to make a man's decisions and is being judged like a man for it. I tried to be there for him when no one else would. I hope all who matter understand that his situation is unfair and I had to do something. We can't keep living high and pretty and be offended by the ugliness in other's lives and not do anything beyond complaining to make it better. The whole world is letting the best of itself fall through the cracks.

Never felt blacker,
Howard

Dear Ms. black juj,

Sorry that happend. I should just bet him up then but he was bigger. My momma a girl. She was nakid and bet up before by men. I got my rib hurt. Rom was beting my family to and that is not rite. Why he get to do that? I want to go home. Mr. Howard to skinny to fight him and you polices. I wish he was bigger, but I like him alot. Rom was beting us and you beting me on my inside chests. Are you sorry?

Sorry, take me home

Not sorry. Wrong

David

Individual Session Details

Service Facility:	2600 Venables Way, Miami, FL 33143
Date of Service:	October 17, 2009
Service Provided:	Psychotherapy
CPT Description:	90901
Place of Service:	Office
Session Notes:	Client has apologized for hostile behavior in initial session, which included throwing chairs and demanding that he be the one to "ask all the questions." Client's wife reports that client has lessened prolonged instances of holding his breath and resumed eating regularly. Crying spells, sleeplessness and an inability to concentrate have subsided somewhat. Client continues to carry a ping pong ball.

Client finally admitted to the letter he had left in the tray of his printer on October 16th was a suicide letter. Client admitted that flash drive he wore on a chain when wife had come home from picking up client's former professor (Victor Lovelett) from airport on that same day was the files of a journal he had been writing for her to find (they had found client in his car parked in the closed-in garage with the engine running, that client was not "trying to find his cell phone in the car" but intending on killing himself by carbon monoxide). |

Client admitted to not blacking out during altercation with homicide victim. Client stated that Roman got him in a headlock and slammed him to the ground. Client attempted to get back upright. Roman slammed client back down and drove a knee into client's side. Child yelled out to mother to hurry and that Roman was hurting client's ribs. Roman began to punch client. Client fought back and heard what sounded like a book being slammed shut. Roman stopped swinging as if he had forgotten something and then pawed at his left shoulder. Client noticed a red dot on Roman's T-shirt at the top of the left shoulder Roman was looking over. Client looked over and saw child at the open front door with gun in hand and aimed at Roman. Roman howled, cursed and lunged after child, who shot the gun again. Roman yelled and gripped his leg. Client could hear mother screaming and coming down the stairs. Roman stumbled at the door, cursing and yelling. Client pulled Roman by his shirt out of doorway and shouted for child to get back in the house and close the door.

Child's mother grabbed child, pulled him inside and closed the door. Roman pulled himself up to his feet and banged on the apartment windows. He cursed at child's mother and told her she had done this to him. Client told Roman he had several minutes to get away and never come back. Roman hobbled toward counselor. Roman's eyes reddened as he whispered that all he wanted was some respect. As Roman limped off, counselor noticed that he had a gun tucked in the back of his pants all along.

Client knocked on door and told mother and child that Roman was gone. Mother opened the door. Client looked down at child, who sniffed and stroked gun as though it were a "pet hamster." Mother grabbed at gun. Child held on to it and told her to leave him alone. Client told mother to back off. Mother stated that client's eye was getting puffy and that she would go into the kitchen for some ice. Client took gun from child, shook child and then hugged him. Child patted client on the back and stated, "You can still see me now 'cause you didn't do it." Client sighed, squeezed gun in order to put his prints over it, and said, "Yes. Yes I did."

Counselor asked client about his feelings for child. Client began to rock in his seat. Client stated that he had been having anxiety attacks since his wife shared with him that she desired to have children. Client stated that "ridiculous dreams full of blue babies that just hissed and stared" at him began around the same time. Client complained that "she" wouldn't leave him alone no matter what he did. Counselor asked who client was speaking of in particular. Client stated that accidents happen, that people should not be judged for accidents. Client explained that boys like to play and sometimes accidents occur. Client shrank in his chair and stated that it was his late infant sister in the dream. Client explained that his parents would leave him with his infant sister on occasion while they ran off for errands on Grand Ave. Client stated that he played his game with a plastic bag where he would place it over his sister's head and "hold her neck a little" to see her "turn blue a little and kick a little or something. She never seemed to do anything."

Client insisted that he did not mean to do it. Client stated that he prayed, did "the church thing" and even held his breath sometimes when alone in his hospital room (deemed as a suicide attempt), home, and office until he blacked out to make amends.

Counselor suggested client consider meditation and focus on breathing to help calm his nerves. Client lashed out that he knew that and for counselor not to try "that ****" with him. Client said he sensed something was wrong and had placed the bag in the trash. Client said it was ruled as "crib death," or SIDS (Sudden Infant Death Syndrome). Client said his mother sees women at the malls and such that would have been his sister's age and still starts "rapidly blinking and flinching if you touch her." Client said his father took to coaching little league sports and would "practically power walk" out of the house to games as though he hated to be in the house.

Client said that he had avoided West Grove, his old neighborhood, out of guilt and shame but was "starting to get better with that." He said he could never tell his parents what he did to his sister and that, "as a shrink," he knows that counselor can never tell anyone either. Client stated he has tried to "get better" by being a mentor to a child who, ironically, wound up killing someone. Client handed a picture of a drawing of Metal Man (a comic character created by client and child). The picture was drawn by client. Client said child's situation made sense, that child should be left to enjoy his childhood. Client pointed to picture and said that "funny, raggedy lil' boy" was enough of a hero to be honest about his struggles and no one could help him, "and here I am, this punk *** mentor that can't be honest about anything and I get a pass for what I did."

Client complained that child is being put through the hell that client should be in. Counselor reiterated client's own words, that client's "situation" with sister was an accident and that client was a child at the time. Client began to weep and complain that child was the protector of his family, what a real man is, while client was "a sickness" his family needed to be protected from. Client stated that "the worst" of it is that child has been flooding his office phone with messages to talk with him because client didn't have the guts to give him his cell phone number.

Counselor asked if client would ever share this with his wife. Client said he did and is in fear of doing anything wrong with his newborn (which has been confirmed as a girl). Client said he had as yet to tell his parents and that the news of a grandchild "means the world" to his parents so he feels that he is "stuck." Client says the only thing that frees him is helping David "Lil DAP" deal with the courts, possible sentencing and lack of family support. Counselor asked client if he had shown as much interest with the upcoming birth of his own child. Client kissed ping pong ball and said sort of, that he had been doing the "Lamaze" class with his wife, but admitted he could do better. Client said he wanted to communicate better with his wife but that she locks herself in the bedroom at night like he is some sort of "disease" and won't speak to him. Counselor suggested client write wife a letter to discuss his concerns.

Tiff:

I hope you read the stuff on the flash drive. The car thing was stupid. I get it. I didn't think things through. This whole thing about what I did to Karen was a big reason why I don't open up a lot. If I never opened up a lot in the first place, then it would not hurt as much when you discovered what I had done and rejected me anyway – like you're doing. Just like you said you wouldn't do. They all say that.

I didn't share what I did with high school girlfriends. I did not start with really being haunted by it until college, when this dating thing started hinting at engagements and marriage and kids, when girls started wanting to know everything. Or so they claimed.

I had a girlfriend in college that said the same open-up, why are men so retarded feminist rhetoric so I told her what I did on the way to the Tallahassee Mall. I finished telling the whole thing as I pulled up with her at this stop light off Tennessee Street. She broke up with me before the light turned green. She paused, looked out of my car window and just got out in the rain and stood on the curb. She started shaking her head and saying it wouldn't work. She called a friend to pick her up, wouldn't even get back in the car. A year and four months, gone. Instantly.

After college wasn't any better. Michelle, the girl I was dating before you, started to not return my calls after I had a few beers and ran my big mouth while we watched some stupid movie about a kid called "Fresh" while we were at her place. I actually liked the movie. Being rejected angered and depressed me. I started feeling like I didn't deserve a decent job, or a college education. Or happiness. I felt like I only had the right to function.

I wanted to make sure I never got into another situation where a child would be close enough to me to even be at risk, so I went in for the appointment for the vasectomy. That is when I met you.

You started quickly talking about relationships, and moving in, meeting relatives. I felt rushed. I don't talk much in general, and definitely not as much as you, but wanted your affection. I needed it. I hated myself for needing it, knowing where it would lead. You wanted to push things to know where it was going. I wanted to slow things down for the same reason. I hated when you said you loved me, because it felt like I was forced to say it back, which reminded me that I do love you, and that you really couldn't possibly love me as much because you don't fully know me.

I knew where this would lead to, regardless of what you were saying. I've planned on the day you would leave the day you came into my life. I don't want you to go. I never wanted you to. I bonded with David because I too, am tired of the broken promises. I'm tired of being rejected. I cannot let you, my daughter or him, down. I need to keep a relationship with him.

Do I make sense to you now?

Howard

October 18, 2009

Tiff:

I got your note. You're hilarious. I pick you up from the hospital and you say nothing but slip notes in my purse. Check your email.

8:12 p.m.

I'm up talking with Lovelett. We just bought the baby some bedtime books at Barnes and Nobles. Thank you again for making his stay comfortable. I'm thinking of quitting 5000 along with the in-home counseling. They'll be pissed at work since they helped get me in. Are you still at Starbuck's?

8:15 p.m.

Tiff:

Stay with 5000. And really, who do you think suggested them to your boss? Lol. Now read your email. There's pizza in the fridge for you and Dr. Lovelett.

8:20 p.m.

I love you.

8:48 p.m.

October 18th
Howard:

I suppose this is a fitting occasion for an old-fashioned, printed letter. Yes, I know I talk a lot. Yes, I did say I was in it for the long haul with you, that my devotion to you was untested. I guess it's always easier to proclaim devotion when the struggle is far off in the distance. I read that journal on your thumb drive. I'm not leaving, but I'm not saying this is easy either, especially since this child has me out of breath and feeling fat and pathetic. I can see you laughing right now, saying of course it isn't easy, it wouldn't really be a struggle if it was. Again, you're right.

You're so much a part of me that I even consider/write your opinions into my own messages to you. You call me out on my BS. You take a lot, and now I know why, but eventually you come around and clear the air. I'm beyond pissed off about all of this and have not wanted you to touch me lately but I know when you hold my hand it cools my brain.

Although I am horrified by what happened, I amaze myself with only being worried over your well-being at the end of the day. When this baby gets her little spinning class going at night and I want to call you in the room to feel her moving, I hear you and Dr. Lovelett talking in the living room or you typing on your laptop when you can't get to sleep on the couch. I call myself fearing for this baby's safety around you, but this fierce, masculine protection you have for David, this need you have to be there for him, cancels the fear out and makes it so that I can only get back to sleep by crying for you. For us.

I know some sort of dark cloud was over you. I've known for years. What was even more maddening was not knowing what it was about while knowing it would possibly destroy the life I had built with you. Were you on the down low? Did you have some kid across town and promised the mother you'd only have kids with her? Were you a pedophile? A habitual liar? Strange enough, your sorrow over your sister was one of the main things that made me love you and tolerate not knowing. I thought, how bad could whatever it is be if any sign of disappointment on his parents' faces tears him apart? How bad could it be if the mere thought of his departed infant sister makes him sigh wearily, fuss like an old man over everyone's safety and be the youngest and only black neighborhood watch volunteer? Your insistence to be there for David, even when things are clearly not in your favor with me, makes me admire and adore you. By the way, a friend at work's husband said Florida has some kind of law called "Stand Your Ground" that says if someone's attacking you with the threat of deadly force, you can respond with such force to defend yourself. He's an attorney. I wish the best for David, but there are concerns I have about him being in our lives that need to be addressed.

What kind of back and forth drama does keeping the relationship with David going leave us open to with the mother? It still rocks me to my core to know you were willing to throw your life away in order to protect him as if not caring how it would affect us. Will you cherish, fight for and protect me and the baby the way you do for David?

  - Tiff

October 18, 2009

Read it. We can work it out. I cherish and love you and the baby. Here's some more love to sweeten the sugar in your Herbal Infusion tea.

9:15 p.m.

Tiff:

Lovelett must be over there teaching you some game.

9:18 p.m.

He can't teach me what I remember that you like. Love you infinity. Come home. It's late.

9:43 p.m.

I love you. Come home. It's late. Don't let me come up to Starbucks and embarrass you.

10:08 p.m.

Tiff:

I'm coming!

10:12 p.m.

October 18, 2010

Roderick Nathaniel Franklin:

I got the little $75 check your momma wrote for you for David's Xmas/birthday gifts. It's so messed up that you can't even call or write to see bout your own son. That boy spent his birthday in juvie hall refusing to come out of his cellroom. I know your momma told you everything that happened. Even locked up like this, your son is shining. He cannot understand much of all of this, but the man in him made decisions when the rest of the world didn't. He know what he did was right no matter what the court do. David is a man. Your ten year old son you left for white folks to pick at label and lock up is a man.

David tries to do what's right even when he don't get help for it. Now I know why you can't see bout him. He more man than you are. If you looked into his eyes, it would rip your voice out your throat. He is not like you at all. He don't just give up on people cause its convenyent. He on a level you aint reached so you have nothing to teach him. He even outshine me and I am woman enough to admit it.

I know I'm mostly why he in this. I'm praying on it. I didn't lay down with a man I admired, but I'm making up for it by giving birth to one.

His shine bought smart, clever people into his life that I could never find for him on my own. They can give him things he need better than I can, but whatever I can do, I'm gone do. I bet he go to college to. The prosecutor say they gone probably let him out tomorrow because they said it was justifiable defense. He will have no record and be everything he supposed to be.

He held my hands when I visited and say he pray he get SIDS. I cry harder than he do and tell him to hold on. You know what he did? He said he was sorry for saying that, for being upset after everything done to him! We got him in this mess and he pologize for lettin' it depress him! Even when he's down, he is more man than you and to stop the child in him from hurtin, I told him that so he can see why you not in his life. Even if you ball this up and don't finish it, you already know it. I just wrote what you already know in your soul.

Sharia

October 19, 2009

Sharia:

They say due to interest of justice, they gonna let him go today. Thank u Jesus! They won't put a weapons charge on him either. No record, no nothing. He free. I need a ride to get him from juvie at 5 oclock. Can u take me?

9:12 a.m.

Yes. Let me text Tiff.

9:14 a.m

They're going to let him go on all charges. He's going to be let out at 5. Sharia needs a ride to pick him up. Me and Lovelett were going to ride there with her to get him.

9:17 a.m.

Tiff:

I'm coming.

9:19 a.m.

You're pregnant. You don't need any more stress.

9:20 a.m.

Tiff:

You noticed. I'll get off early. I need to meet David and Sharia. I need to meet them for myself.

9:22 a.m.

Okay. I'll send you the address.

9:25 a.m.

Victor Lovelett

I'm back in Tallahassee. It was good to see you even with the circumstances being what they were. Tiffany really loves you, Howard. I know you know that but I felt I would be negligent to not say so. Her meeting Sharia went well. When she met David and he asked if he could touch her belly and she let him, man, I could really see this all working out.

Oct. 21

Howard Capelton

Yeah, I know. The big thing was when she offered to drive them back to their apartment and we followed behind them.

Oct. 21

Victor Lovelett

Yeah, they all needed time to talk.

Oct. 21

Howard Capelton

Thank you. I understand how Sharia feels. I feel unbalanced with gratitude. If there's anything I can do for you, promise me you'll let me.

Oct. 21

Victor Lovelett

Fight for your family, extended family included. Fight to forgive yourself.

Oct. 21

Howard Capelton

I knew you'd go all altruistic on me. All that is common sense and seems easy enough.

Oct. 21

Victor Lovelett

Okay, reach out to your parents. I'm not talking some Apple-pie-all-American-good-son-bought new house or material thing. They need you, front and center. When your parents came over to the house later that night and you finally told them what had happened with Karen, for some reason, I wasn't surprised when your father looked at me and said he suspected what had happened all along.

Oct. 21

Howard Capelton

But he said you were my father all along. What kind of nonsense is that? It's like he gave me away!

Oct. 21

Victor Lovelett

Like I was saying on the way back to the airport, it explains the sudden distance he kept with you afterwards and ever since, the rushing out of the house to coach football to other children, while leaving you with your mother. He was saying that since there was distance between you two, someone had to be some sort of father figure for you in his absence. He recognized that I had been that person. He was saying that I had been looking out for you all this time while he was struggling with what his intuition was telling him.

Oct. 21

 Howard Capelton

Guess I should have just been happy with the whole fight for David and Tiff and the baby offer.

Oct. 21

 Victor Lovelett

It explained the silence you sensed between your parents when he said whenever he brought up the possibility of what happened to your mother, she would shut down. When your mother started crying and locked herself in his car, it dawned on me that she feels guilty for having left you with such a young child for such a thing to have happened. You say it was just a half hour that she went off to the grocery store, but to her, it must feel like she left you for days alone with Karen.

Oct. 21

Howard Capelton

And then there's West Grove. There's therapy, for me. There's so much to do.

Oct. 21

Victor Lovelett

When you are a man forever trying to grow, yes. No struggle, no progress.

Oct. 21

Howard Capelton

I'll let you know if anything else comes up.

Oct. 21

Victor Lovelett

Please do. I'll send some money this weekend for his birthday gift. I'm looking to come down and see how you guys are when the baby arrives.

Oct. 21

Howard Capelton

You saved my mind. You saved my life.

Oct. 21

Victor Lovelett

Our people are waiting. Let's go save some others.

Oct. 21

November 15

Mr. Capelton:

I fully understand, with the recent events involving your client, your reasons for resignation. I hope and pray for you and your family, as well as for the client and his family. We will again offer his mother counseling, as we offered her earlier. It is our hope that she takes advantage of it, seeing that attempting to cope with such trauma without professional attention can lead to further complications and painful, avoidable events in the future for not only her but her son as well.

Your concern for your client has touched our hearts, Howard. Your step beyond the comfort of the numbers and policy of the insurance field was courageous and inspiring. I sincerely want the best for you. Although the state's proposed requirements are pushing you and others out of in-home counseling, I am confident I will cross paths with you and others of your quality in the future. Perhaps an administrative position in in-home counseling is in your future. You have a life-affirming gift.

_____

Eudonis Warner,

Lead Counselor

423 NW 27th Terrace

Ft. Lauderdale, FL 33313

Sunrise Family Services

305-***-****

Nov. 25 2009

Dear Ms. Tiffany,

Thank you for a good Thankgiving dinner. Thank you for saying sorry for all that happened to me. Nobody but Mr. Howard and momma said that before. When you did I felt better. So I call you ma-am then. Thank you for letting me come and eat your food and being my friend. Let Mr. Howard come over sometime. Momma said he can.

Mr. Howard say he will play me more jenga when he see me. I beat him every day when he visit me in the day room. Mr. Howard daddy and momma was very nice too. He look like them. You like how I say grace? Mr. Howard showd me how to pray. I did not want to, but it was okay.

I don't want no gang. I don't want to hurt nobody. I don't want to get hurt either. I never want that but it just keep happening. I just want to be a boy. I want to be funny and strong. I just want everybody to anser my questions sometimes. I am just a boy.

Thank you, ma-am

David Troy aka Little DAP

Dade County Gazette

Happy First Birthday:

Korinne Sankofa Capelton,

Born June 19, 2010

Daughter to Tiffany and Howard Capelton

William Hobbs

Discussion Questions:

1. What do you think of Howard's feeling that it was pointless to train David up in a manner that David's own mother could not fully appreciate in the men she dated?

2. What do you feel about Howard's complaint that black men who have no criminal background are not considered cool or interesting enough to be listened to by the youth?

3. And, on the other hand, since no one is perfect, how "perfect" must someone be in order to be a role model?

4. How important do you think it was that Howard face a violent confrontation in order to gain David's respect?

5. Consider the issue between Howard and David concerning manners. Do you think there are some rules of survival that people who live as nicely as Howard cannot possibly understand concerning children like David?

6. What do you think of mentoring systems that reward the child's good behavior by ending the scheduled interactions with the mentor?

7. Do you think it is necessary to share extremely personal aspects of your life to someone younger than you in order to help them through a situation?

8. What are your thoughts about the way Howard handled his secret – especially after so many people abandoned him after hearing of it?

9. Explain why Roman was either a thug or just misunderstood.

10. Howard's mission was to help David become a less violent person, yet David wound up killing Roman. When looking at all of the surrounding circumstances, did Howard succeed or fail?

11. What do you think of Lovelett's insistence on Howard respecting the honor of those he sought to help? Which is more of a problem, that or people expecting assistance while doing little to nothing for themselves?

12. If Sharia remains single, do you think there will always be tension between her and Tiffany?

13. What do you think of the importance of Dr. Lovelett in this story?

14. What will be the boundaries you draw between sustaining your family/household and helping someone in need outside of it?

15. Many believe anyone who does not volunteer any of their time and energy to the community should not have a right to complain about the community's condition. Are there any exceptions to this rule? Should there be?

16. How can a child like David survive his neighborhood while not falling victim to limiting his life to the stereotypes that cripple black males?

17. How much does Metal Man have in common with most young boys/men?

18. How important is it to have both Howard's book knowledge and David's street knowledge?

North of the Grove

19. What is the most important scene in this story and why?

20. Where would you imagine the characters of this book to be by the time Korinne reaches David's age?

40483135R00148

Made in the USA
Charleston, SC
03 April 2015